THE DAYS OF THE RAINBOW

ALSO BY ANTONIO SKÁRMETA

The Dancer and the Thief (2008)

The Postman (Il Postino) (1987)

the days of
the rainbow

•

Antonio Skármeta

Translated from the Spanish by
MERY BOTBOL

OTHER PRESS • NEW YORK

1 3 5 7 9 10 8 6 4 2

Billy Joel, "Just the Way You Are," from *The Stranger* (1977),
Columbia Records.
Los Prisioneros, "La voz de los '80," from *La voz de los '80* (1984),
Capitol Records.

Library of Congress Cataloging-in-Publication Data

Skármeta, Antonio.
[Días del arcoíris. English]
The days of the rainbow / By Antonio Skármeta ; Translated from the
Spanish by Mery Botbol.
pages cm
Originally published in Spanish in 2011 as Los días del arcoíris by
Planeta Publishing.
ISBN 978-1-59051-627-0 (pbk.) — ISBN 978-1-59051-628-7 (ebook)
1. Chile—History—20th century—Fiction. 2. Dictators—
Chile—Fiction. I. Title.
PQ8098.29.K3D5313 2013
863'.64—dc23
2013008403

TO

Roberto Parada Ritchie and his family

TO

Manuel Guerrero and his family

TO

Raúl Alarcón

Erano i giorni dell'arcobaleno,
finito l'inverno tornava il sereno.

Those were the days of the rainbow,
When the winter ended, clear skies returned.

—NICOLA DI BARI

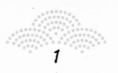

1

ON WEDNESDAY, they arrested Professor Santos.

Nothing unusual these days. Except that professor Santos is my father.

Our first class on Wednesdays is philosophy, followed by gym class and then algebra for two periods.

We normally go to school together. He makes coffee and I make fried eggs and put the bread in the toaster. Dad likes his coffee strong with no sugar. I have mine with a lot of milk, and even though I don't use sugar either, I stir it as if I do.

This month the weather is bad. It's cold and it drizzles, and people cover their noses with their scarves. Dad has a light-colored raincoat, beige, like the ones detectives wear in the movies.

I put my black leather jacket on top of my uniform. The raindrops slide down over it, and I don't get wet. The school is only five blocks away. As soon as we get out of the elevator, Dad lights his first cigarette and smokes it slowly until we get right to the school door.

He makes his cigarette last exactly that long, then he throws the butt to the ground and makes a theatrical gesture so I crush it with my shoe. Then he goes to the teachers' lounge to pick up the class book, and when he gets to our classroom he asks where we left off last time.

Last time we were discussing Plato and the allegory of the cave.

According to Plato, men live like zombies watching moving images on the wall of a cave, images that are nothing but the shadows of the real things outside projected by a fire against the wall. Those men, who have never seen the real things, believe that these shadows are real things. But if they came out of the cave and saw everything in plain sunlight, they would realize that they had lived in a world of shadows and that what they thought to be true is only a pale reflection of reality.

Professor Santos takes attendance before getting back to Plato, and if a student is absent he puts a red dot next to his name. Although we walked to school together, when he gets to S, immediately after "Salas" he says "Santos," and I have to answer, "Here." My father argues that the coincidence of having to take philosophy with him does not release me of any of my responsibilities, even the absurdity of having to answer the roll call. He says that if I don't study, even though I'm his son, he'll fail me.

I like philosophy, although I wouldn't like to be a teacher like Daddy because then I'd have to get up early in the morning, smoke black cigarettes, and, on top of all that, I wouldn't make much money.

Before starting the lesson, my father brushes off his lapels just in case he dropped ash on them. And then he says his favorite phrase: "Why is there Being rather than Nothing?" And adds: "That's the million-dollar question. And that is, after all, the only question and the big question of philosophy."

The question that worries me lately is that, if there is Being, there must be a meaning for it, because if there were no meaning, it would be irrelevant whether or not there was Being.

My girlfriend, Patricia Bettini, says that the meaning of Being is just being; that's it, without any purpose of any kind. She asks me not to complicate things so much and to be more spontaneous. She's kind of a hippie.

That very Tuesday night, before they arrested him, I explained to my Dad Patricia Bettini's thoughts, and he got outraged. He put salt twice in his soup and then he pushed it to the side and said he wouldn't eat it because it was too salty.

I turned on the TV, but the first image was of Pinochet kissing an old lady and I turned it off before Daddy could see it.

He then used the occasion to tell me that I shouldn't trust Patricia Bettini so much because if she thinks that Being is nothing more than what Being is being, she's missing something that no intelligent girl would ever forget, that men have consciousness, that men are Being and, simultaneously, they think about Being, and therefore they can give Being a meaning and a direction. That is to say, they can set values and can aspire to those values. Goodness is goodness. Justice is justice, and there is no such thing as "justice as far as possible."

According to my daddy, what matters most is ethics, that is, what we do with Being.

2

ON THURSDAY AFTERNOON, Adrián Bettini got a letter. It was not delivered by his usual mailman but by two young officials with police badges under their lapels. They rang the bell briefly and smiled to the maid while they asked to hand deliver the letter to the owner of the house. The young Nico Santos, invited that day to have tea with the family, watched the scene from the dining room and then noticed the look that Patricia Bettini gave him when her father, with a casual and uncomplaining stride, went to the door dressed in a discolored wool coat.

After signing and writing his ID number on the notebook the two unconcerned young men gave him so that he could sign for the document, he opened the envelope and immersed himself in its contents.

As if guessing that his daughter and Nico would ask him about the missive, Mr. Bettini told them it was a subpoena from the Department of the Interior to report in person tomorrow at 10:00 a.m. at General Pinochet's government office.

Patricia Bettini couldn't help being surprised. Her father had been in jail twice, and he had been kidnapped and beaten unconscious once by some unidentified thugs.

The man asked his wife, Magdalena, to join them at the tea table, and after stirring his teacup for a long while, confessed that he didn't know whether to attend the meeting with the dictator the following day or immediately pack some clothes and hide in some of his friends' houses for a few days.

Patricia Bettini recommended that he hide.

His wife recommended that he attend the meeting. It was better to face the situation than to live in hiding.

Nico Santos carefully spread guacamole on his toast. The silence was so deep that even that slight movement of the knife over the piece of bread seemed raucous to him.

3

AND THEN IT HAPPENS that on Wednesday we were discussing the allegory of the cave when two men with short hair and clean shaved walked into the classroom and asked Daddy to accompany them.

My father looked at the chair where he had left his raincoat, and one of the men told him to take it with him. My father took it and didn't look at me.

That is, I don't know how to explain it, but he looked at me without looking at me.

And it was weird, because when the two men took my daddy with them, all the other students in the classroom were looking at me.

I'm sure they thought I was afraid. Or they believed I should have jumped on the men and attacked to prevent them from taking my father.

But Professor Santos and I had foreseen this situation.

We had even given it a name: We called it the Baroque situation. If they took Daddy prisoner in front of witnesses, that meant they couldn't make him vanish like they did to other people, people who are put in a bag with stones and are thrown into the ocean from a helicopter. There are thirty-five students in my class and we all saw with our own eyes that they took my father. He says that that's an optimal situation, because they won't kill him. In cases like this, he's protected by the witnesses.

According to the Baroque plan, when they take Daddy prisoner I have to make two phone calls to two numbers I learned by heart, although I don't know the names of the people who are going to answer. Then I have to keep living a normal life, going home, playing soccer, going to the movies with Patricia Bettini, going to school as usual, and at the end of the month, I have to go to the treasurer's office to pick up his paycheck.

So when they took Professor Santos, I began to trace circles on a piece of paper while I felt silence growing around me like a spiderweb. I'm sure that my classmates thought that out of sheer instinct I should've jumped and defended my old man.

But my father has told me a hundred times already that he isn't afraid of anything in the world except that something bad happens to me.

And everybody around here knows that a seventeen-year-old boy disappeared months ago and he isn't back yet.

I have to ignore those looks because I can't explain to my classmates that I'm applying the Baroque syllogism.

If they had made my father disappear without any witnesses, we would be facing the Barbarian syllogism, and I would've probably died already of sadness.

After they took Professor Santos, Inspector Riquelme came and gave us a reading-comprehension exercise.

And when we finally got to recess, I went to the restroom. I didn't want to talk to anyone. I didn't want anyone talking to me.

4

MR. BETTINI dug up a tie from a trunk and knotted it unenthusiastically in front of the mirror. He sent his daughter, Patricia, in a cab to school and asked his wife to go with him up to the gate of the presidential palace. Once there, he kissed her, and after getting out of the car, he gave her the keys to the vehicle, "just in case."

At five to ten, Adrián Bettini entered the dictatorship's central headquarters.

The receptionists in the lobby were dressed in fuchsia uniforms, spoke softly, were polite and smelled good.

They took him from one office to another, from one elevator to another, from one officer to another, until finally they made him sit in an office with soft leather armchairs and quiet carpets.

Behind the desk ("behind the desk," Bettini said to himself, as if he were telling someone the story that he was never going to have the chance to tell), the minister of the interior himself was sitting.

Bettini was about to faint. Dr. Fernández was considered the regime's toughest man. Only General Pinochet beat him in these matters.

He knew, even in his strict silence, that if he had to speak right at that moment, his voice would come out hoarse.

The minister of the interior smiled at him. "Thank you for coming, Don Adrián. I want to inform you that in two months the government will call a plebiscite. Why are you smiling?"

The man tried to hide the grimace on his lip. Then he closed his hands tightly inside the pockets of his jacket and answered, "A plebiscite like the one in 1980, Mr. Minister?"

"The 1980 plebiscite was not fraudulent. Pinochet won with seventy percent of the votes. But I understand all too well that, in view of such strong evidence, you, being a leftist, would resort to demagogic clichés and accuse us of fraud."

Bettini brushed off his lapels as if he wanted to remove an ash. Arguing face-to-face with the minister of the interior was making him feel unexpectedly calm. If they were going to kill him or torture him, anytime, whatever he could say would be irrelevant. A sort of sudden suicidal dignity filled his mouth faster than his thoughts.

"I'm sorry if I gave you that impression, Mr. Minister. But people tend to think badly when there are no other legal parties represented in the voting booth, when the ballots are counted only by members of the government, when there is no electoral commission, and when there is no independent press to write about any political opposition. But aside from these tiny details, the plebiscite that Pinochet won back then must have been fair."

The minister swiveled in his armchair and smiled, showing perfect teeth that made him look younger.

"This time, everything will be done to perfection. We want our October fifth plebiscite to be irreproachable and unimpeachable. Members of the opposition will be allowed to be at the voting tables, there will be delegates of our political enemies working at our computer centers, we won't ban international election observers, and as of tomorrow, martial law will be lifted throughout the country."

"Sounds good! And what are we going to vote on?"

"*Yes* or *No*."

"*Yes* or *No*?"

"*Yes* means that you want Pinochet to stay another eight years as president. *No* means that you want Pinochet to leave and to have presidential elections, with several candidates to choose from, one year from now."

"Elections!"

"And that's not all. Since we want to democratically legitimize Pinochet in the eyes of the entire world, we're going to allow the opposition to campaign for the *No* to Pinochet option on TV."

"On TV!"

The minister offered him a glass of fizzy mineral water.

"I don't have any champagne here for you to celebrate. But please have this glass of cool water."

Bettini's mouth was so dry that he rinsed it discreetly before swallowing.

"Well, Mr. Minister. Congratulations on these democratic outbursts. Can I ask you now why you summoned me?"

The official got up from his armchair with a solemn and indecipherable gesture, and caressed the tassels that adorned the curtains of his large window.

"I know you're a bitter enemy of our regime," he told Bettini, with his back to him. "I also know that, on one occasion, some of my men taught you a little lesson."

"A lesson? What a notable euphemism, Mr. Fernández!"

The minister turned around and waved a finger in front of Bettini's nose. "For your information, I severely reprimanded them for that."

"My broken collarbone thanks you. Now, can you tell me what you want from me?"

Fernández brought his hands together and put his fingers over his chin.

"Fifteen years ago I was working as a top executive for Coca-Cola and I got to admire you as our competitor's advertising agent, when you came up with a commercial for a new soft drink called Betty, which had a funny taste, a bitter flavor. It was very difficult to introduce such a bitter-tasting beverage to the market because back then everybody was used to sweet sodas. Remember?"

"I remember, Mr. Minister."

"Do you remember the slogan of that successful campaign?"

"Yes. Betty, a bit bitter, like life."

"Brilliant, Bettini, brilliant!"

"I can't believe you summoned me just to congratulate me on a slogan I wrote fifteen years ago!"

The minister rubbed his right fist against the palm of his left hand.

"No. But now I have to sell a product that people consider bitter—another eight years of Pinochet."

Bettini didn't know whether to smile or to look undaunted.

"Mr. Minister, what are you proposing to me?"

"Since I assume that the opposition will hire you as the creative director of the campaign for the *No* to Pinochet option, I'm offering you the position of head of the advertising campaign for *Yes*."

"*Yes* to Pinochet?"

"*Yes* to Pinochet. I'd have expected any reaction from you to such a proposal but a smile. Believe me, I feel relieved. Why are you smiling?"

Patricia Bettini's father pressed his nose with three fingers as if he wanted to ease a pain.

"Life takes so many turns! When Pinochet led the coup and made you one of his ministers, I was fired from my job, sent to jail, and tortured. And now, the same person who sent me to jail and laid me off is offering me a job."

"I'm aware of the paradoxical nature of this situation. But you're the best advertising agent in the country, and for this campaign I want only the best. A professional! You might criticize our government as much as you want, but you can't deny that we have a brilliant team of professionals. Our economy's flourishing!"

"For the rich."

"But the time will soon come when there will be so much wealth that it will trickle down to the poor."

"There you have the slogan you need for your campaign: 'When the wealthy have enough, they'll throw the banquet leftovers to the poor.'"

"I'm confident that you'll come up with something better, Bettini. What do you say?"

"What do I say? I say that they say that nothing that happens in this country escapes you."

"Oh, yes. I've heard that exaggeration too."

"They say that not even a leaf falls without your consent."

"My fame sometimes pleases me and sometimes makes matters more difficult for me."

Bettini filled his glass with mineral water, took a sip, and wiped his lips with the back of his hand.

"My daughter, Patricia, is worried because your men arrested her boyfriend's philosophy teacher."

"I see."

"He's an old man, an expert in Greek philosophy. He's a threat to no one. Just an old guy."

"So old that he sold toffee at the Roman circus?"

The minister stroked his legs, celebrating his own joke with a burst of laughter, and then opened a green file cabinet.

"He's not young anymore."

"Forgive my joke, Bettini. Many people worry for no reason. Sometimes my men ask a couple of routine questions and then the detainees can go back home as if nothing had happened."

"Mr. Minister, more than three thousand people are missing."

"Those statistics are an exaggeration! The country has already overcome the crisis. Didn't I tell you that we're going to call a hundred percent democratic plebiscite? Your daughter doesn't have anything to worry about."

Bettini stood up and touched the knot of his tie to hide the movement of his Adam's apple while he swallowed the saliva accumulated in his mouth.

"Santos," he said hoarsely.

"Pardon me?"

"Santos. The philosophy teacher's name is Rodrigo Santos."

The minister put his hands on top of the file cabinet and, smoothing a piece of paper, traced a circle with his ballpoint pen.

"School?"

"National Institute."

"Wow! 'The nation's first spotlight.'"

"Excuse me?"

"'The nation's first spotlight.' That's what the institute's anthem says. Where did the events take place?"

"The classroom."

"Witnesses?"

"More than thirty students. They were in the middle of class."

The official sighed with a sudden air of fatigue.

"Physical appearance of the officers?"

"Short hair, young, raincoats . . ."

"Like in the movies. Date?"

"Wednesday. Last Wednesday, early in the morning."

The minister closed the folder with a blow while lifting his chin. After a long silence that seemed full of meaning, he started to talk again.

"So, Bettini, what can you tell me about our business?"

"Our business," the ad agent said to himself. So he had something in common with the minister of the interior. "Our business."

"How long can I think about it?"

"You can take a couple of days."

"I'll call you on Monday, then."

"Don't worry about it. You'll come in person. I'll send a couple of guys to bring you right here."

"See you on Monday, Dr. Fernández."

The minister stood up and held out his hand to say good-bye.

"Philosophy. I remember a bit from my school years. 'I only know that I know nothing.' Who said that?"

"Socrates."

"And the other thing about the river?"

"Heraclitus. 'You cannot step into the same river twice.'"

"See you, Bettini."

5

I CALLED the first number but nobody answered. This was the phone number where supposedly there would always be somebody to answer. If nobody answered, it would mean that the person who should've answered had been taken prisoner.

So I dialed the second number.

Someone answered. Following the rules of the Baroque syllogism, I did not ask who was there, nor did I identify myself. I only said that Professor Santos had been taken prisoner. The man on the other end of the line said that he would take care of it.

He asked if there were any witnesses.

"Of course there were. There are thirty-five of us in the class, and I'm the thirty-first in the roll. That's because of the S. The S in Santos."

"Fine, then," said the man. And he repeated that he would take care of it.

I know perfectly well what it means to take care of someone in a case like this. The man will go to see the priests, one of the priests will talk to the cardinal, the cardinal will talk to the minister of the interior, and the minister of the interior will say to the cardinal, "Don't worry, I'll take care of it." According to the Baroque plan, I don't have to do anything else, because if I go to the police, they may arrest me, and if that happens, then for sure my old man will go mad.

So that Wednesday, I go back home and see the two plates for lunch that had been set there that morning on top of the blue-and-white plaid tablecloth. Next to Dad's glass there's a small carafe of red wine, half full, and next to my place, the bottle of apple juice.

I sit at the table. I don't feel like going to the kitchen to warm up the stuffed potatoes left from the night before. I stay there for half an hour not knowing what to do and unable to think about anything. Every time I try to start thinking, I grab my fork and hit the empty dish.

At last, I go to my bedroom and lie down on my bed and read the sport magazine *Don Balón*. My favorite team, University of Chile, is not doing well. The problem's that when the team has a good player, they sell him to another country, Spain or Italy, and so the team gets weaker.

It's cold and the electric heater's unplugged. Dad says it uses too much energy and his salary's not enough to keep it on all winter. I cover up with the blanket.

6

"SO?"

"My answer is no."

"Bear in mind that the compensation would be very good."

"Just out of curiosity, how much is it?"

"You tell me. There's no limit."

Bettini looked at the wall behind the desk. There was a color picture of the dictator and nothing else competing with his presence.

"Actually, this is the best offer I have ever received. It makes me really mad to have to say no, especially when I'm still out of work."

"A star like you still out of work!"

"Advertising agencies have a black list of professionals, issued by your office, in which it's 'recommended' not to hire me."

"My goodness, Bettini! How do you make a living?"

"My wife has a job, and I make a few bucks writing jingles under a pseudonym."

The minister moved his neck for a while as if to show a sort of supportive surprise and indignation. He put his finger on his lower lip and stroked it repeatedly.

"Okay, Bettini. So what do you say?"

"I thought a lot about it. Thank you, Mr. Minister. But I can't accept it."

"For moral reasons?"

"Yes, sir. For moral reasons."

He stood up and straightened the edge of his jacket.

"But right now your behavior's not moral at all. It's not ethical to reject someone's offer based on political differences. What if a doctor refused to help someone who's sick only because the patient's his political enemy. Would you call that ethical behavior?"

"Honestly, sir, if the patient were Pinochet, yes, I'd say that's ethical."

The minister walked to the window and drew the curtain a little. Santiago's grayish smog was right there, punctual and tenacious.

He talked to the advertising agent in an abrupt voice and with his back turned to him.

"I'm sorry that I can't count on your services, Bettini. It'll be a tough campaign. Thank you for coming."

He kept looking out the window, without turning around. But Bettini remained still until the minister was forced to turn and look at him.

"Anything else?"

"Yes, sir. I came here trustingly because you sent for me. I'd really like to leave this place in the same way I came in. You know what I mean . . ."

The minister smiled broadly and then burst into loud laughter. "I guarantee it."

"Thank you."

"You're welcome."

He walked toward the door, but his own steps on the soft carpet pushed him down and held him back. The relief he felt when he reached the door was abruptly interrupted.

"Bettini."

"Sir?"

"If you want to give me a thrill, don't agree to lead the campaign for the *No*."

"That's okay, Mr. Fernández."

"Good-bye, Bettini."

7

THE DOORBELL RINGS. According to the Baroque plan, it cannot be my father because he has the key. If it were the cops, they would be coming either for me or to search Daddy's desk. I jump up and check what he left on his table. There's a document addressed to the minister of education, Mr. Guzmán, requesting that our school—the school where he teaches and I study—no longer be led by a military officer. It also says that the presence of that officer at the nation's oldest school is an insult to teachers' dignity and goes against freedom of speech. On top of the page, the manifesto reads, "We, the undersigned . . . ," but the only signature on it is his—Professor Santos. I wad up the document and throw it out the window.

The doorbell rings again and I put on my coat. If they're going to take me, I'd better go well wrapped up. I'm very sensitive to cold. During class recess I always look for the sunny walls and I shrug my shoulders as if by doing so I could accumulate heat. When at last I open the door, the person who's there, with her finger still pressing the doorbell, is Patricia Bettini. She comes and hugs me. Then she says, "My poor dear love."

She asks if I have had lunch. I tell her that I hate stuffed potatoes. She goes to the kitchen and makes an omelet with oil, eggs, cheese, and tomatoes. She cuts the omelet in half. I put salt on mine and dip a piece of French bread in it. She doesn't use any salt because she says that salt makes you gain weight. She has a lot of theories about how to lead a healthy life; she refuses to put salt or butter in her food, and she's a great fan of Ionesco's plays. She played the role of Ms. Smith in *The Bald Soprano*. Anyhow, everyone's name in *The Bald Soprano* is Smith. But now, after graduating from high school, she's going to study architecture, not drama.

"We have to find your father," she says.

"But how?"

"Asking everywhere for him."

"I already did what I had to do."

I explain to her the whole Baroque syllogism. She listens carefully and shakes her head.

"In cases like these, good people cannot do anything, because they're all afraid. We should try to make the others do something."

"The bad ones?"

"Nobody's one hundred percent good or completely bad."

"My father thinks that you have no principles and that an ethical person must have principles."

"I do have principles. My principle's that I love your father and I love you."

"Those are not principles. Those are feelings."

"Okay, then, my feelings are my principles."

Patricia Bettini does not answer. She takes a cassette tape out of her purse and plays it in the Sony cassette player. It's Billy Joel, and the song is "Just the Way You Are." It's in English:

> *Don't go changing, to try and please me*
> *You never let me down before*
> *Don't imagine you're too familiar*
> *And I don't see you anymore.*
>
> *I wouldn't leave you in times of trouble*
> *We never could have come this far*
> *I took the good times, I'll take the bad times*
> *I'll take you just the way you are.*

8

ADRIÁN BETTINI'S WIFE didn't want to turn off the headlights or move the car from the parking space reserved for members of the government until her husband came back from his appointment with the minister of the interior. That's what she haughtily and clearly told the captain who, with excessively courteous manners, asked her to move her car. While he used his cell phone to contact Fernández's office, she twirled her wedding ring around her index finger until the metal seemed to be burning her fingertip. When the guy in uniform was walking away, she saw Adrián coming, so she quickly turned on the engine, as if they were fleeing after robbing a bank.

"How did it go?" she asked while driving around Italia Square and checking the rearview mirror to see whether someone was following them.

"See for yourself. I'm alive."

"Did he insist that you work for the *Yes* to Pinochet?"

"Of course."

Even though the light was not red, Magdalena stopped the car, ignoring the horns of all the cars behind her.

"So?"

Bettini smiled. Trying to imitate Fernández's resounding voice, he said in his deepest possible tone, "Right now, your behavior's not moral."

"But where did he get the idea that you might work for them?"

"Some computer might have told them that I'm the best ad agent in the whole country."

"Of course you are."

"In spite of the total consensus between my wife and that computer, nobody gives me a job. Do you want me to drive?"

The honks of the cars behind were getting louder and louder, so Magdalena set off at once.

"And finally, what did you tell him?"

"No, thank you."

"Were you polite?"

"As much as I was able to be."

"And what did he say?"

"'That I could give him a thrill by refusing to lead the ad campaign for the *No*.'"

Now it was Magdalena who kept smiling for a long while.

"As soon as it was announced on the radio that there would be a plebiscite, Don Patricio called to offer you to lead the advertising campaign for the *No*."

"Oh, my God!"

"You have to accept it. I'd be so proud of you if you did it."

"Magda, if I accept, the minister won't be thrilled. And you know what that means."

"If you were the advertising director for the *No*, your visibility would protect you. The government cannot pretend they are calling a democratic plebiscite and kill the director of the opposition's advertising campaign."

Bettini rubbed his eyes. Everything seemed so normal and real. However, he still had a slight hope that it was all just a bad dream.

"I must admit that you have a point. Even so, there's another reason why I shouldn't accept it."

"Tell me."

"Pinochet has been bombarding the country with advertising for fifteen years and I would have only fifteen minutes on TV. It's like the battle of David and Goliath."

"Adrián."

"What?"

"Who won?"

"Who won what?"

"The battle of David and Goliath."

Bettini fell back onto the seat and covered his ears with both hands. In the last year, Magdalena had gotten into the habit of stopping the car every time she thought she had said something clever. Now Bettini didn't know what was upsetting him most—her words or the honking of the cars behind them.

9

TODAY'S MONDAY. The sky's covered with black and gray clouds, but it's not raining. The city of Santiago feels heavy on people's necks and everyone walks fast with their heads bent down. I barely slept last night, and now, as I walk to school, I yawn ten times per minute. Our first class is history; then we have philosophy.

That means that I'll have the chance to sleep at my desk. When I get to school, I remember Dad again. I wonder if he has cigarettes and if he's allowed to smoke. I see a butt on the floor and I smash it with my shoe.

When it is time for our philosophy class, we enter the classroom all at once, without lining up first in the corridor. A couple of classmates pat me on my shoulder and I wrap my blue scarf around my neck. It's freezing cold. To avoid having to talk with the boy next to me, I take out my pencil case and start sharpening a pencil with my metal sharpener.

Then the philosophy teacher comes in.

He's not Mr. Santos. He's a young man with thick eyebrows and turned-up nose. He wears round glasses like John Lennon's and a shiny blue blazer. He's very slim, and as if to show his strength, he lets the attendance book fall on his desk with a thud. Then he opens it, clears his throat, and starts taking attendance.

After saying each name and hearing the word "Here," he looks up and makes an affirmative gesture, as if he already knew the students. When he calls "Santos," I stand up, but he doesn't make that affirmative gesture—he keeps his eyes fixed on the attendance book. Then he looks up again—32, Tironi; 33, Vásquez; 34, Wacquez; and 35, Zabaleta.

He takes a piece of chalk from the edge of the blackboard, tosses it up and catches it without looking at it. That gesture makes him look even younger. Then, he says, "My name is Javier Valdivieso, like the Valdivieso champagne. I have seen Professor Santos's notes and I know that you have already studied the pre-Socratics and Plato. So today we'll start to study Aristotle. Aristotle's ethics. Write this down: 'None of the moral virtues arises in us by nature, for nothing that exists by nature can form a habit contrary to its nature. For instance, the stone that by nature moves downward when we drop it cannot be habituated to move upward, not even if one throws it up ten thousand times, for it would end up falling down ten thousand times.

"'The virtues, therefore, arise in us neither by nature nor against nature; rather, human beings possess a natural aptitude to receive them and perfect them by habit. That way, by performing just actions we become just, and being afraid or acting valiantly in front of danger makes us either cowards or brave.'"

And then he says, "On Wednesday, we'll have a quiz on Plato and the allegory of the cave."

10

BEFORE ADRIÁN inserted the key, Magdalena opened the door for him from the inside. She kissed him energetically on his cheek and made a gesture with her head toward the living room.

The opposition leader, Don Patricio Olwyn, was smiling at him with an expression that seemed cut from the same cloth as Jack Nicholson's.

"Coffee, Senator?"

"Thank you."

"Sugar, Senator?"

"That's fine. And don't call me 'senator,' I beg you. Since those beasts closed the Congress, what's left is just my longing for that title."

"And what brings you here, Don Patricio?"

"Something big, something that can become magnificent."

"Tell me about it."

"For the October fifth plebiscite, Pinochet is going to authorize the opposition to do a fifteen-minute campaign against him on TV."

"Really? That's amazing!"

"The election is thirty days away, and our ad must start broadcasting next week."

"There's no time for anything."

Bettini touched the pocket of his shirt and was about to take out a cigarette when he thought that it would be impolite to smoke in front of such an important person. He kept the box between his hands, caressing the cellophane wrapper.

"That's the dictator's strategy. Strike fast, so the enemy doesn't have a chance to react."

To place more emphasis on his words, he stood up.

"My friend Bettini, on behalf of the sixteen political parties that have agreed to vote against Pinochet, I came to offer you the leadership of the advertising campaign for the *No*."

Adrián Bettini stood up as well and, with a gentle gesture, asked his wife and daughter to leave the living room. Still, he was able to read what Magdalena's lips were saying behind her smile: "Go ahead!"

Once he was alone with Don Patricio, Bettini replied, with no tact whatsoever, "How much are you paying?"

"The pay is . . . well . . . it's *ad honorem*."

"What do the polls say?"

"Ours? That the *No* could win."

"And theirs?"

"That the *Yes* wins."

"And what do you think?"

"I don't know. But I can assure you that our polls are not embellished to please ourselves. In Chile, there's a lot of unrest and anger against Pinochet, and that unrest represents the feeling of the majority. The problem is that this plebiscite will be determined by those who, as of today, are undecided."

"Are there any undecided people in Chile today, after fifteen years of terror?"

"Pinochet has convinced everyone that if he loses, Chile will go to hell. He appeals to those who don't have good memories of the overthrown Socialist government."

"You were an enemy of that Socialist regime, and one of the Christian Democrats who promoted the riots that led to the military coup."

"This is not the time for blame. You and I are now in the same team—against Pinochet!"

Bettini let himself fall on the couch and, somber, kept his eyes fixed on the coffee he hadn't even tasted. At the same time, Don Patricio sat courteously and turned his head, observing Bettini expectantly.

"I'm happy to hear that. But there is a reason why I cannot accept your offer."

"Explain yourself!"

"The coalition that supports the *No* is made up of sixteen political parties! It's such a broad conglomerate that it's impossible to think it has its own identity. And advertising a product requires being able to define the product with total clarity. Success is not achieved with ambiguities. There are so many parties behind the *No* that I don't even know them. And you?"

"There are sixteen, plus the Communists, who support us but are not part of the coalition."

"Could you list them?"

"Well, there is us, the Christian Democrats, then the Socialists, the Social Democrats, the Liberal Party, the . . . Can I now say 'and so on'?"

"And you expect me to come up with a clear advertising concept from such disparate movements?"

"If we didn't know that you're the best, we wouldn't have turned to you."

The advertising agent got up, victim of a sudden itch that made him scratch his neck. He drew the curtains and looked at the snowy peaks of the Andes.

"Chile's such an odd country! Even though I'm its best ad agent, I've been laid off in a country where everything's advertising. Because I'm a good ad agent, I get threats, I'm sent to jail, they torture me, then throw me to the street again, branded as an agitator. When I'm offered a job I cannot accept, it's the best salary in the world. When I'm offered a campaign I should accept, it's *ad honorem*."

The senator went to the window and put a fraternal hand on Bettini's shoulder.

"Your personal experience perfectly matches the public situation. A fierce dictatorship that took power with cannon shots, air raids, torture, prison, terror, and exile decides to stay in power not by force but with the Versaillesque gesture of calling a plebiscite. And on top of all that irony, it offers its opponents, for the first time in fifteen years of complete censorship, fifteen minutes on TV to convince the people to vote against the dictator."

"They're going to legitimize themselves internationally as a democracy."

"And the only way to prevent that from happening is if the strategy backfires on them. That is, Mr. Bettini, if you make the *No* win. What do you say?"

Bettini closed his eyes and rubbed them vigorously as if to get rid of a bad dream.

"My dear Senator, I don't hold out any hope for the triumph of the *No*. I don't think that this country, ideologically poisoned and terrified, will dare to vote against the *Yes*, and I haven't the slightest idea what the slogan of the campaign could be."

Don Patricio patted Bettini's shoulder affectionately once again, and raising his thick eyebrows, smiled and said, "That's a good beginning. Do you accept, then?"

Over Don Patricio's shoulder, Bettini was astounded to see his wife giving him the thumbs-up from behind the half-open door.

"Okay, Senator, here you'll have the Chilean translation for the Japanese word 'hara-kiri'—I accept."

The politician hugged him, then put on his hat left the house in a rush, just in case Bettini changed his mind.

From the window, the advertising agent saw the senator getting into his car. He also observed that, as soon as the senator's car left, another car left behind his.

He decided not to worry. As long as he didn't appear publicly in the campaign, the minister of the interior wouldn't be unhappy. As for Don Patricio's safety, he should be okay—at least until the plebiscite took place. If what Pinochet wanted right now was to legitimize himself as a democratic ruler, he couldn't have the leader of the opposition killed. That was Magdalena's good point. But that would work only in a rational country, not in one where arbitrariness rules.

Now he did allow himself to light a cigarette and exhaled the first puff sitting at the piano. He didn't come up with a song to promote the *No*. Instead, as soon as he touched the keys, an ironic circus tune came out of his fingers. Then, like the great Garrick, laughing so as not to cry, he improvised a few verses:

> *I'm the Superman of advertising.*
> *One day I'm here, next day I'm not.*
> *One day I sell handcuffs, next day I sell*
>   *freedom.*
> *I die today with laughter, tomorrow I'll be*
>   *shot.*

> *I'm the Superman of advertising.*
> *If it doesn't rain, they hit me*
> *and if I make it pour, they hit me as well.*
> *Even if they say they love me, they all hit me.*

Magdalena came into the studio and leaned on the piano.

"So?" Adrián brushed the ash off his lapel and, taking a deep puff of the cigarette, closed the black lid.

"David and Goliath," she said.

11

AFTER SCHOOL, I don't feel like going back home and stay on the street corner. When Dad's not home I don't keep things tidy. I don't do the dishes and let everything pile up in the kitchen.

I try to remember the phone number of the guy who would talk to the priest. He would probably have some information already. But I shouldn't call him from home. I wait for the pay phone at the bus stop to become available. I rub the hundred-peso coin until the metal gets warm.

That's what I'm doing when Professor Valdivieso approaches me.

"A cup of coffee, Santos?"

"What for?"

"For the cold, I think."

We walk up to Café Indianápolis and lean on the counter looking at the waitress's bottom wrapped in a miniskirt two sizes too small. When they bring us the steamy coffee, the teacher puts his hands around the cup to warm them up, and I pour so much sugar that Patricia Bettini would surely disapprove.

"Santos," he says, "this is not an easy situation for me. It's not my fault that I have to teach you in the class that your father was teaching."

"It's not my father's fault either."

"I accepted the job not to make your father's life more complicated but because life must go on. Our children have to get an education, no matter what."

"An *ethical* education," I say.

"I don't care what kind of political opinions your father may have had."

"Well, they're nothing special. His fundamental conviction's to fight against Pinochet."

"Do you see? Your father shouldn't mix a political situation like the one the country's going through with the philosophy of Plato, who lived two thousand years ago."

"Professor Valdivieso, I don't know what you're talking about."

He takes a sip of coffee and gets some foam above his upper lip, which he wipes off with his sleeve. I see that the pay phone has just become available and squeeze the coin in my pocket.

He takes a folded piece of paper out of his jacket and flattens it on the metal counter. It's a handwritten text. He reads it aloud, but comes closer to me, and in a confidential tone: "'We can then say that Chileans under Pinochet's dictatorship are like the prisoners in Plato's cave. We're looking at sheer shadows of reality, misled by a TV that's corrupt, while brilliant men are confined to dark prison cells.'"

"Where did you get this, Professor?"

"These are the notes of one of your classmates, Santos. The student handed them over to the principal."

I stir my coffee so briskly I spill it all over the saucer. Behind the cashier, there's a shelf with cigarettes of all brands. The black tobacco my father smokes is there, too.

If I only knew where he is, I'd bring him a pack.

"Santos, I hope you won't hold a grudge because I've taken your father's position."

"Not at all, Mr. Valdivieso."

"You know that this is Chile's best school, and that, for a young teacher, getting to work here's something to be proud of and an asset in his professional career."

"Don't worry about it."

"The thing is that I would rather have gotten here under different circumstances. For example, through a public examination, instead of having been handpicked by the principal."

I bring the cup to my mouth and blow on the coffee. It's still too hot. I put it on the counter and pour the coffee in the saucer back into the cup.

"If you had not accepted the job," I say, "someone else would've."

"That's the problem, Santos. Before calling me, they had offered the job to Dr. Hughes and Professor Ramírez. Why are you smiling, young man?"

"Your class on Aristotle, Professor Valdivieso, was really good. My father's a great fan of the *Nicomachean Ethics*. That's why he calls me 'Nico.' Because 'Nicomachus' would be a little too much."

The man takes off his John Lennon glasses and rubs his eyes.

"By the way," he says, "I'll see how I can compensate in some way the harm I'm causing you."

"No, Professor. I beg you not to worry. I'm okay. I'm great."

But when I finally make that phone call, I'm not okay anymore. I'm not great at all.

The priests don't know in what cell Professor Santos had been thrown.

12

IN THE AFTERNOON, Adrián Bettini ended up in downtown Santiago. In that mixture of bank clerks, store managers, financial executives, and secretaries wearing too much makeup and miniskirts so short they provoked long gazes from men, he believed he could feel the truth of a city destroyed by violence.

From downtown, everyone went back to their neighborhoods, either rich, middle class, or a poor housing area. Downtown offered them the chance to be in physical contact where all the differences of a country so sharply divided seemed to dissolve. At night, there wouldn't be any amusement for them other than watching TV. There, unless the dictator changed his mind, his own fifteen-minute show would appear, encouraging that defeated mass, wrapped in worn-out coats and frayed scarves, to vote against Pinochet. The way they drank their coffee, in silence, at Café Haiti, letting their absent gaze slide down the waitresses' hips, was a good sign of apathy.

On the front page of *La Segunda*, below the newspaper's green logo, a headline in red print stood out: OCTOBER 5 PLEBISCITE. But nobody was buying the newspaper. Only he stopped to read a subheading in bold, "The *No* Campaign Is Authorized to Be on TV."

He used to run into friends from the advertising industry in that café. Or journalists. Nowadays, most of them had left the country, and all that his lively old-days café friends were doing now was discussing soccer and the ups and downs of the exchange rate. These men would be some of his campaign's target group. Rather than inscrutable, their faces seemed to be uniformly expressionless. It wasn't because of fear, but because of their simple daily lives emptied of all hope. They had their coffees in a long ritual designed to delay going back to their offices, where they would stare at their computer monitors with someone else's numbers and products. Exactly that, like someone else's, their lives didn't concern them at all.

He arrived home late. On his desk, he found Magdalena's message: "Warm up the stew in the microwave." There was a bottle of red wine, unopened, and several bread rolls, not so fresh. He poured himself a glass of wine and, without knock-ing, entered Patricia's room.

In the semidarkness, he saw his daughter sleep-ing with an arm around the pillow. He turned on the soft light of the table lamp and stayed there, look-ing at her for a while. Who could teach him how to make her happy? He regretted the hard years when trying to survive without a steady job made him ac-cept temporary positions that didn't leave him any time or money to give his little one. He could barely make the Scuola Italiana's monthly payments, and even that, only with a burdensome loan.

He talked to her in a soft voice. "Patricia, wake up."

The girl sat up abruptly in her bed. "Anything going on, Dad?"

"I'm sorry, dear. But I have to ask you some-thing important."

"Tell me. What is it?"

"What are you going to vote for in the plebiscite?"

"And you wake me up only for that, Dad?"

"Please, answer me. What are you going to vote for?"

"No!"

"What a relief! At least one person is going to vote *No*."

"No, Dad. You misunderstood me. I'm not going to vote *No*. I'm just not going to vote."

Bettini swallowed. He wished he had a glass of water.

"Why not?"

"We have already discussed that many times at school. I want to go back to sleep."

"But it's very important that you tell me now."

"Why?"

"Because I've just accepted the ad campaign for the *No*."

"Oh, Dad, you're crazy!"

"Yes, we agree on that. Now, tell me why you're not going to vote. I need that information. Professionally."

"Because Pinochet will commit fraud. No dictator calls a plebiscite to lose it. Because the politicians who are in favor of the *No* are a jumble of groups that have no idea of how to lead the country if they win. Because I'm convinced that this country has no way out. I don't believe that a dictator who came to power by force of arms could be overthrown by putting little papers in a ballot box."

"What do the other students think?"

"The ones in lower grades, who are under eighteen, don't vote. In my class, they think like me."

"They all think the same way?"

"No. The usual cuckoos think that it makes sense to vote *No*."

"Like me."

"Like you."

"Then what are you going to do?"

"What do you mean? What am I going to do for what?"

"To end the dictatorship. To put an end to Pinochet."

"Nothing."

"Patricia!"

"Why are you so shocked, Father? Instead of wasting my time doing cheap politics, I'm going to get good grades, I'll apply for a fellowship, and I'll go as far away from this country as possible. I'll leave it all to Pinochet and his ass kissers.

Bettini got closer to the lamp, and Patricia could see his astonished expression.

"So you don't have any courage to fight?"

"What for, Dad? Look at yourself. You haven't had a job in years. Everybody says wonderful things about you, but just like they would say wonderful things about someone who's dead. About Napoleon, for example! Times have changed. The rules of the game have changed, too. I find your moralistic attitude very nice but totally naïve."

The girl raised her hand and caressed the man's cheek.

"I see," he said.

"Am I hurting you with my words, Dad?"

"No, no."

Slowly, Bettini moved away from the edge of the bed. He felt as if the ceiling had fallen onto his shoulders.

"Don't leave so sad, Father. I love you a lot."

"I know, my dear."

"And it's important to tell the truth to the people we love."

"I agree."

Right at the moment when Bettini was about to open the door, the girl jumped out of bed and hugged him tightly.

"Dad?"

"Patricia?"

"If you lead the campaign for the *No*, then I'm going to vote *No*."

13

PATRICIA BETTINI is kind of a hippie, but she doesn't want to have sex with me before we graduate from high school. She sees the end of high school as a moment of liberation. She thinks that all good things in life will come together—going to college, having sex, and, of course, the end of Pinochet.

It's like when Catholics make a vow. She got it into her head that if she can hold on for the next six months, she'll get a great score on the aptitude test, get accepted into the architecture program, and Pinochet will be overthrown.

Last Tuesday we were supposed to get together, but she didn't show up. Later that evening, I called the same number and a voice said, "I'm sorry, kid, we have no news about your father." On Wednesday, early in the morning, it's drizzling again, like last week. Some buses go through the Alameda

Avenue toward Barrio Alto, where blue-collar workers, maids, and gardeners go to work at the rich people's houses. The smoke from the exhaust pipes rises
and mixes with the stagnant gray air.

Nobody seems to be doing anything to change
the situation. They are paralyzed, just like me.

Actually, I obey my dad. He's a philosophy
teacher, and if he said that we're in the Baroque
syllogism, I believe him. While I'm at the school
gate, staring at the sidewalk looking for a lit cigarette butt to smash, I have a brief daydream. I'm
walking into the classroom a little bit late, and Professor Santos is taking attendance, and when he
calls my name, I say, "Here."

I'm a little late, but I get to class in time to
get a piece of paper with questions that Professor
Valdivieso is handing out. He wants us to explain
how one can ascend, according to the allegory of
the cave, from the world of shadows to the bright-
ness surrounding the ideas.

My classmates work in silence, filling in the
first page fast.

I hear the paper rustling every time they turn
the page to write on the other side. I know the alle-
gory of the cave by heart, and Dad and I have read
Plato's dialogues a few times. He plays Socrates and
I play the other character, but instead of answering
I keep on thinking about Patricia Bettini, about

Dad's raincoat, the one he took from the chair the morning they came for him, and about the lyrics of Billy Joel's song, "Just the Way You Are."

Five minutes before the class ends, I think I was able to remember the entire first stanza of Billy Joel's song. I write it down in Spanish on the test page, while I sing it in English:

Don't go changing, to try and please me
You never let me down before
Don't imagine you're too familiar
And I don't see you anymore.

I wouldn't leave you in times of trouble
We never could have come this far
I took the good times, I'll take the bad times
I'll take you just the way you are.

I don't write anything at all about the allegory of the cave.

"How are you, Santos?" Professor Valdivieso asks me when I hand him the test.

"Still here," I say and walk out to the schoolyard amid my classmates.

14

WHEN BETTINI LEFT the place, he was determined to tell Olwyn that he was going to quit. After all, the sum of factors yielded the same product: a demoralized population, acceptance of the dictatorship, discouragement mixed with tedium, isolated heroic acts of resistance crushed by the regime, not even one bright idea to start the campaign, and Dr. Fernández's voice resounding in his head like a bitter warning: "If you want to give me a thrill, don't agree to lead the ad campaign for the *No*."

He entered Olwyn's office without a greeting so that he wouldn't have to regret it.

"I cannot think of anything," was the only thing he said.

"How come?"

"This country's emotionally devastated by Pinochet. People feel hopeless. I resign."

"Your task is to come up with a campaign that would give them courage."

"Courage! They see everything gray!"

"Think of a strategy that would make them see the future in a different color. I'm sorry, but I cannot waste my time with you right now. I have to work my butt off to keep the sixteen political parties that are with us together, to keep the coalition from breaking apart, and you dare to come with your little metaphysical quibbles?"

Bettini let himself fall in the old leather sofa. "I feel so lonely, sir!"

"But why? The Chilean people and sixteen political parties are on your side!"

"I'd rather have just one opposition party with a clear identity, instead of this jumble."

Olwyn struck a hard blow on the table. He seemed to have lost his patience. "'Jumble'! Where did you get that word, Bettini?"

"From my daughter, sir."

"From your own daughter?"

"Yes, sir, my own daughter."

"By Saturday, at the latest, I need the logo for the *No*, the jingle for the *No*, and the poster for the *No*."

"Yes, sir."

"What are you going to do now?"

"I'm going to have a whiskey."

"You're a genius! Couldn't you think of anything at all?"

"Just stupid things. Things like 'Democracy or Pinochet.'"

"What a bore!"

"Instead, I came up with a good one for the campaign in support of Pinochet, 'Either me or chaos.' It has all the precision that we don't have. Besides, people don't want freedom. They only want to consume. They look at the commercials, totally captivated, and get into debt so they can buy everything. And Pinochet tells them that if he loses, the shelves will be empty."

Olwyn stared at him while rubbing his hands together, like a priest.

"Would you feel more comfortable working for the *Yes*?"

15

THE VOLUNTEERS who wanted to testify about how they were enduring the dictatorship gathered in the studios of Movie Center Productions—mothers of disappeared children, women who had been raped, teenagers who had been tortured, blue-collar workers with kidneys beaten to a pulp, deaf old people, jobless men and women who had lost their homes, students thrown out of the university, pianists with broken wrists, women whose nipples were bitten by dogs, office clerks with absent looks, hungry children . . .

A fifty-year-old woman accompanied by a guitarist approached Bettini. "I want to dance a cueca on your TV show."

"A cueca is fine," the advertising agent said. "It's something cheerful."

"This young man's my son, Daniel. He's a guitarist."

"Hi, Daniel."

"This cueca is for my husband, a missing detainee."

"Whom are you going to dance the cueca with?"

"With him, sir. With my husband."

She pulled a white handkerchief out of her blouse, and holding it with her right forefinger and thumb, waved it delicately. The boy played the first strums, and in a high-pitched voice she sang the first verse: "My dear, there was a time when I was happy . . ."

The fact that the woman responded to her missing husband's dance steps in such a decent, simple way made her dance even more devastating. Bettini made a vague gesture to excuse himself and went to the restroom.

He let the water from the sink run over his neck, not caring if he was sprinkling his shirt, and rubbed his face under the faucet as if he wanted to wash away his pallor.

His tears, too, dissolved in the sink.

16

AFTER HIS FIRST WHISKEY there was a second one, and he softened the third with so many ice cubes that the glass overflowed.

In between sips, he played a few arpeggios that distracted him rather than helping his imagination focus. The aversion he felt for the political apathy of the Chilean people was so strong that he wondered whether President Allende's suicide, in such a pusillanimous country, had really been worth it. What was left of all the energy of the seventies? Just tons of skepticism, a somber burden that prevented them from flying.

On TV there were only game shows, old stars hoping to make a comeback, bolero dancers in effeminate sequins, plummy voices announcing that a street in Ñuñoa had been recently paved.

And commercials.

The frenzy of advertising—apartments, lingerie, jeans, lipstick, chocolate milk, perfume, bank loans, mattresses, supermarkets, sunglasses, wine, tickets to Cancún, private colleges. The ads were much better than the soap operas and the pop singers.

No wonder! All his friends in the movie industry who had been laid off were now making cameo appearances for advertising agencies under pseudonyms. People were used to that. And that's what he should use to advertise *No*. Present it as a tempting product, like strawberry ice cream or French champagne, like a vacation package to Punta del Este, a Falabella suit, or a crispy rotisserie chicken.

At the dinner table, he talked to Magdalena about it. His wife listened, rolling crumbs from the bread basket into balls. Finally, she could not keep quiet anymore, and brushing off the tablecloth with the palm of her hand, confronted her husband.

"The *No* to dictatorship is not a product. It's a profound moral and political decision. You have to convince people that their dignity is at stake. You were always an ethical person. Don't sell out now."

Bettini raised his voice, too. "I know that the *No* is not a product. But in order to convince people, Pinochet has been advertising on TV for fifteen years. I get only fifteen minutes to convince the 'undecided' to vote against him. I have to encourage the Chilean people to buy something that's not yet in the market."

"What is it?"

"Joy! Let's start with a drawing, a simple image that could be the campaign poster."

He extended a white poster board on the tablecloth.

"Let's take it one step at a time," his wife proposed. "That simple image, what should it convey?"

"The drawing must show at first glance that there are sixteen political parties that are very different from one another but have united to win."

Magdalena took the black felt-tip pen and drew a sketch on the poster board.

"A hand. What do you think? There are five fingers, but they make up one hand. It gives the idea of unity and diversity at the same time."

"Hmm. There are some fingers missing from that hand."

She changed the image. "Then let's have two hands shaking. Ten fingers."

"But all those fingers are the same color."

Magdalena poured India ink on the board.

"A white hand and a black hand."

"Who's going to look at it? This is the only Latin American country where there are no black people."

"Look at this—a hand squeezing a tube of paint."

"Not bad. But a hand squeezing something is a fist. A fist may please the Socialists and the Communists, but not the Liberals or the Christian Democrats."

"Let's forget about the hands. The text that goes with the image, what would it say?"

"*No.*"

"Just that?"

"The *No* will be better alone than in bad company. Everybody has to have a reason to vote *No*, and the poster should be broad enough."

"It must be more explicit, Adrián. 'No more torture,' 'No more poverty,' 'No more missing people,' 'No more exile.'"

"Oh, *nooooo!* Don't come to me singing the same sad tango we have being dancing all these years, please. The new thing must be joy. The promise of something different."

"Frivolous and banal."

"My broken collarbone appreciates your compliments."

"You don't have any principles."

"But I have goals. And my goal's to make the *No* win. And I can assure you that with your pathetic militant and melancholic help I won't get too far."

"What do you need, then?"

"Joy. Light at the end of the tunnel."

"How can we make something positive out of a negative word? The *Yes* campaign has it made: 'Yes to life!' 'Yes to Chile!'"

"I need a break. Give me a breather. I need a miracle."

The doorbell rang, tinkling like a Christmas sleigh bell. Both turned toward the clock on the wall, and they kept looking at it with their question hanging from their jaws.

When the doorbell rang again, Magdalena pulled her hair back, tied it with an elastic band, and walked toward the door.

"I'll open," she said.

17

THE YOUTH of the Pro-FESES movement, who want to unite the high school students of all Santiago, think that the fact that my father's missing is an excellent reason to take over the school, and they have summoned me to a meeting at the library.

I follow my old man's instructions and tell them I don't get into politics. According to Patricia Bettini, this isn't getting into politics because it's about one's father, about one's teacher.

"Not yours," I tell her, wrapping my scarf around my neck.

But I immediately regret having said that, because her father was taken a few years ago and got his collarbone broken.

I know by heart the principles of the high school movement—destabilize the dictatorship by provoking riots. This would give the impression that the country is ungovernable. They also want to unite all those who're against Pinochet—whether or not they belong to a political party—even those who only want to make trouble, just for the fun of it.

We all have taken to saying some phrases in English. We learn them through songs or from our teacher, Rafael Paredes. He's leaving next month for Portugal, because he was hired to make a movie. My old man thinks this is the perfect time for Mr. Paredes to go to Portugal, Greece, or anywhere else in the world, because he knows very well that the cops are after him and all his family.

My old man and the English teacher are very close, even though they have an eternal dispute. They can never agree on who's the greatest man in history. My daddy votes for Aristotle—in whom, he claims, everything begins and ends—and Paredes for Shakespeare. Deep in my heart, I tend to agree with my teacher, Paredes, but how could I be against my daddy?

Of course, both of them are pretty "daring."

It's less apparent in my father, because he's a calmer person. Paredes can be as imposing as an opera singer.

If my English teacher went into hiding, they would catch him in no time. He's more than six feet tall and has a deep voice that resonates against the school's old walls every time he walks into the classroom. He teaches in the mornings, and nights he plays with a group of actors. He's sort of impressive, that's why he always plays kings, commanders, or ministers. When he walks into the classroom, he throws the attendance book on his desk and delivers lines from Shakespeare's plays. We have to memorize and then interpret them in writing, and hand in the paper the following day.

The last one was, "Stars, hide your fires! Let not light see my black and deep desires." We have to squeeze our brains to guess what Shakespeare meant by it. What happens is that Macbeth is eager to be king, and the fastest way is by assassinating the king himself. Just like Pinochet, let's say. But it's not easy for him to make up his mind, even though his wife eggs him on. She's even more wicked than Macbeth.

Professor Paredes calls Shakespeare "Uncle Bill."

Actually, that's the last quotation to be included in the English test we'll have after the opening of *The Cave of Salamanca*, and Paredes has promised us that he'll be "compassionate" when grading them if we do well in the play.

After the test, he'll say good-bye to the school until October, provided that he's allowed to come back to Chile, because the movie he'll be filming in Europe is somehow "daring."

A "daring" movie is one that's not going to please the regime.

The weather in Santiago's still pretty bad. The drizzle sticks on our cheeks, and the smog makes us cough. We take shelter at the bus stop on the corner to smoke cigarettes, with no desire to go home yet.

Next to us there's a boy with long hair and a blue raincoat who catches our attention when he looks in the opposite direction from which the bus is coming. Suddenly, he takes a stack of flyers out of his bag and hands one to each of us in the group. Then he climbs on the first bus leaving and winks at us.

The blue flyer says, "Action," and it has instructions on how to take over the school as a protest in support of the teachers who have been laid off. I believe we all would feel ashamed of throwing the flyer on the ground, so we end up putting it in our backpacks.

18

THE LITTLE MAN who rang the doorbell of the house, making more noise than a train driver, had a head of coarse hair that made him look three inches taller and wore eyeglasses with a thick frame. His mustache fell disheveled over his lips, as if no two hairs rhymed with each other. His outfit didn't look any better—a black suit polished by the years that shone here and there, in contrast with a few wine and ketchup stains, something that Magdalena de Bettini didn't notice at first sight.

"Sir?" Magdalena inquired tentatively, surprised by the man's puzzling appearance.

"Is this Adrián Bettini's home?"

"Yes, it is."

"The great advertising agent Adrián Bettini's?"

"So they say."

The little man bent forward in an old-fashioned bow.

"I need to talk to him."

"What about?" she asks, trying to push the door a little so that the man, on his tiptoes, can't see her husband in the back of the living room.

"It's confidential."

"I'm his wife. You can talk to me in all confidence."

"Confidential, madam, confidential."

"Could you at least tell me on behalf of whom you come . . . ?"

The man cleared his throat while wiping his forehead with a gray handkerchief. Or a handkerchief that had once been white. Another thing that was difficult for her to discern.

"I come on behalf of young Nico Santos. My password is 'Nicomachus.' For more details—the Aristotelian ethics. May I come in now?"

The woman opened the door and the little man slipped in like a lizard. In no time, he was in front of Bettini, who replied to the man's Versaillesque bow with a discreet movement of his neck.

"Mr. Bettini, I presume?" the man said, with a smile that raised his thick mustache up to his nose.

"Yes," the ad agent said.

"It's my pleasure meeting you, sir. My name is Raúl Alarcón, but my friends call me Little Kinky

Flower. I'm five-and-a-half feet tall, and I'm a poet and a composer."

"What can I do for you?"

"Nico Santos sent me. You know him—Nicomachus."

"Well, what is it?"

"Yesterday at school, Nico told me that you're going to undertake the ad campaign for the *No* with a joyful approach, that you're going to tell us all that when the *No* wins, joy will come back to Chile."

Bettini made eye contact with his wife and saw her put a finger to her temple, signaling that their surprising guest had a loose screw.

"That's what I'd like to do. But up to now, I haven't gotten too far. I don't even have the campaign jingle."

"That's the reason why Nico—Nicomachus—sent me to see you. I have the jingle for the *No* that you're looking for."

"Did you compose it?"

"Oh, no. Johann Strauss did. But I wrote the lyrics."

"Sing it, please."

Alarcón moved his head in different directions like pecking the living room with his eyes.

"Piano *habemus*?"

"*Habemus*," Bettini said, sensing that his face had suddenly gone pale.

He led the man to his studio, opened the lid of the baby grand, and invited his guest to sit on the stool. Before sitting, the little man cleaned the plush of the bench with the sleeve of his jacket. He glided his fingers in a pair of scales and inhaled deeply before hitting the keys again in a thundering chord.

There followed a spirited interpretation of "Blue Danube." Then the man stopped abruptly and fixed his gaze defiantly on his host.

"D'ya feel the melody?"

Despite the paleness that was growing on his face, Bettini couldn't help smiling at the colloquial "d'ya feel . . . ," so improper coming from someone who looked like a character from the Spanish Golden Age picaresque.

"I feel it," he said cautiously. "Strauss's 'Blue Danube.'"

"Can you think of a single man or woman in this country who couldn't sing this tune?"

"I doubt it. It's a pretty catchy tune."

Alarcón cheerfully struck his thighs. "Catchy. Exactly. It's very catchy."

"I'm curious to know what all of this is leading up to."

The little man's eyes lit up. "Dude, you're getting into it, aren't you?"

If, awhile before, Bettini couldn't believe his eyes when he saw Little Kinky Flower in his timeless outfit, now he couldn't believe his ears hearing such broad anthology of Chilean slang.

"I'm getting into it, Alarcón. Very much so."

"Now, feel this," he said. He cleared his throat and licked his lips. "Excuse my voice, sir."

"Go ahead."

After a brief and florid piano introduction, Raúl Alarcón, aka Tiny, also called Little Kinky Flower by his friends, delivered the following verses to the tune of Strauss's "Blue Danube."

> *We start to hear now "No, no. No, no"*
> *all over Chile, "No, no. No, no."*
> *There they sing "No, no."*
> *Here they sing "No, no."*
> *Women sing "No, no"*
> *and the youth sing "No, no."*
> *"No" means freedom.*
> *Let's sing together, "No, no, no."*
>
> *For life—"No."*
> *To hunger—"No."*
> *To exile—"No."*
> *To violence—"No."*
> *To suicide—"No."*
> *Let's dance together,*
> *to this "No."*

No, no.
No, no.
No, noooo.
No, no, no.
No, no.
No, noooo.
No, no.
No, no.
No, no.
Let's dance together
to this "No."

No, no.
No, no—

"May I interrupt you for a moment, Mr. Alarcón?"

"Sure, Mr. Bettini."

"I have to make a phone call right now."

"No problem."

"I'll be back in a second."

Bettini dialed Nico Santos's number as if he were stabbing him.

"Nico?"

"Don Adrián!"

"He's here, in my house. Alarcón, I mean."

"Tiny?"

Bettini looked at the man, who made a friendly gesture at him with his hand.

"Yes, Tiny."

"And what do you think?"

"I think that if you ever send me another mad man like him, I won't let you walk into my house again. And I'll forbid Patricia from seeing you."

"But what's the matter, Don Adrián?"

"You know what's wrong? That in this country there's no room for more foolishness. And you sent the king of fools to my place."

"So?"

"So what?"

"Didn't you want joy, Don Adrián? There it is. 'No, no, no, no, no, noooooooooo . . .' I find it awesome!"

Bettini hung up with a somber expression, and with his head hanging down, he walked toward Alarcón, who was eagerly waiting for him.

"So, Mr. Bettini? What do you think about my 'Waltz of the *No*'?"

The ad agent let each syllable drop like a stone from his mouth: "Awesome, Mr. Alarcón. Awesome."

"Thank you. But I only take credit for half of the work. The other half comes from Strauss's talent."

"Alarcón and Strauss."

"A winning duo."

"Strauss and you make a great team."

"Like identical twins."

"As thick as thieves."

"Exactly."

Bettini grabbed the man by his neck and without much effort lifted him off the piano stool. Keeping him up in the air, he took the man to the door and gave him a final push.

"Get out!"

Only then did he realize that Patricia Bettini, holding the key in her hand, had just witnessed the unusual scene.

19

IN GYM CLASS we are jumping over a pommel horse, rolling over the mat, and then running back to the end of the line to start all over.

We're wearing white T-shirts and shorts, and the exercise is not enough for us to overcome the cold weather. We rub our thighs and forearms. The teacher blows a referee whistle every time he wants us to change the pace of our jumps and somersaults. He should be feeling warm in his blue sweatshirt. Next to him, there's a boy about our age. The teacher makes him watch everything we do. After a while, he asks me to make room for him before me in the line.

"He's a new student," the teacher explains to me. "A Chilean who just came back from Argentina."

The student is warming the palms of his hands by breathing into them.

"Where did you come from?" I ask him.

"From Buenos Aires. My old man was exiled there and now he was allowed to come back. They removed the *L* from his passport."

"What's your name?"

"Héctor Barrios."

"And how do they call you? Tito?"

"No. The Chilean."

"Well, start looking for another nickname, because we're all Chilean here."

We run together to the pommel horse, but before jumping he freezes and looks at the teacher in distress.

"What happened, Barrios?"

"I don't know, sir," he says, with a strong Argentine accent. "When I got to the thing there I thought I wouldn't be able to jump over it, I thought."

"The thing there is perfectly designed for an eighteen-year-old young man. Go back to the line and jump."

I go back with him to the starting point.

"I jumped one of those once, and I broke my wrist," he says.

"Okay. Forget it. I'll tell the teacher."

"Thank you. What's your name?"

"Nicomachus. But they call me Nico."

"In Buenos Aires I had a classmate whose name was Heliogabalus."

"And what did they call him?"

"Gabo."

"Like García Márquez."

"Right."

I get a running start, keep running, and neatly jump over the leather bar and roll gently on the mat. Then I go toward the teacher.

"What's wrong with Che?"

"The wrist, teacher. He fractured it pretty badly."

"In Argentina?"

"Poor guy," I confirm.

"You're kidding!" the teacher says to me, and makes a hand gesture asking Barrios to come.

"I spare you this time, Che. In the name of San Martín and O'Higgins's hug."*

Barrios pokes my chest with his finger.

"I knew that in Chile I was going to be called Che."

---

* A reference to the "hug" between Latin American liberators Bernardo O'Higgins (Chilean) and José de San Martín (Argentine), which took place on April 5, 1818. The battle fought that day against the Spaniards would determine the independence of Chile.

20

PATRICIA SAW THE MAN, without even shaking the dust off his jacket, stand up from the sidewalk and leave like a dog with its tail between its legs.

"My God, Dad, what have you done?"

Bettini walked into the house, turning his back to Patricia while she was talking to him.

"I'm trying to write the jingle for the ad campaign, and that fool comes to my house to sing 'No, no, no, no' to the tune of 'Blue Danube.'"

"Did you kick Tiny out?"

"Tiny, but with a foolishness that is inversely proportional to his height!"

"But, Daddy. He sang that song at the Scuola Italiana yesterday. And it's a catchy tune. Today, all the students in my class were singing it."

Bettini stopped abruptly. "All the 'undecided' students?"

"Everyone. That waltz is awesome, Dad."

They walked into the studio and the ad agent cleaned the keyboard with the sleeve of his shirt as if he wanted to erase Alarcón's fingerprints.

"Awesome! That's what your boyfriend Nico Santos told me a few minutes ago."

"But it's true! He also went to our school and played it for the students. He goes from high school to high school, from college to college, singing that song. Students help him hide when the cops arrive."

"It wouldn't be necessary. He's so short that if he wore a uniform, he would pass for a student."

Bettini sat at the piano. He pushed the pedal down for emphasis and played the most emblematic melody of Allende's years: *The people united will never be defeated.*

"I have to come up with a harmony capable of bringing together Liberals, Christian Democrats, Social Democrats, Radicals, leftist Christians, Greens, Humanists, Reborn Christians, Communists, Centrists . . . What a cacophony!"

Patricia stayed with her father until he gently closed the lid of the piano, putting an end to his defeat.

"Don't be so old-fashioned, Dad! If you want to encourage people to vote *No* with joy, you have to compose something really cheerful."

"That's what I'm trying to do. But nothing comes to me."

"A tune with good vibes!"

"Like rock and roll?"

"Sure! Why not? Something light, like the Beatles' music. You have to make people feel that it's cool to say *No!*"

Patricia imitated the neck movement with which Paul McCartney used to follow the beat, shaking his head.

"She loves you, yeah, yeah, yeah . . ."

"Which, in my case, would be, 'She loves you, no, no, no . . .' What the heck will I do with this damn *No?*"

"Something youthful, cute, amusing. Something with a little whoop at the end: 'No, oh, oh . . .'?"

Bettini rubbed his eyes, trying to erase the image of this nightmare.

"No, oh, oh . . . ?"

"That's it, No, oh, oh . . ."

"Good-bye, Patricia!"

"Are you leaving?"

"Nope. You are!"

21

LAURA YÁÑEZ is now at my place. She's Patricia Bettini's close friend and, at the same time, the complete opposite of her. While Pati's a good student and has thin lips, small breasts, and straight brown hair that she wears in a ponytail that she tightens with a barrette, Laura has dark, messy curls that shine with gel. Even in the middle of winter, her skin is copper colored, as if she had just come back from the beach. Her purse is covered with stickers with the images of the new pop stars, and her fleshy lips are enhanced with a vibrant lipstick that she puts on as soon as she leaves the school. Her chest busts out from the uniform shirt, and she unbuttons it enough for us to see the vertiginous curves of her smooth breasts. Her easy smile shows perfect teeth, and she constantly moves her hips as if she were listening to tropical music.

About her school life she says only, "I'm a lion-ess in a cage." This motto's confirmed by her report card, where, by the end of the semester, the grades in red look like a cherry festival.

I make her some tea and don't ask what brings Laura Yáñez by herself to my place, because I pre-fer not to know. Her contribution to "teatime" is a pack of Triton cookies, the round chocolate ones with white cream filling. After the first sip, she tells me she came to ask me for a favor.

She has arrived at the conclusion that even if she burns the midnight oil studying from now on, she'll never be able to make up for those red grades, so she'll have to repeat the year.

"Just imagine," she tells me, "the effect that would have on my mood. All of my girlfriends are going to college, or they're going to start dating so they can get married, and I'd have to stay in that cage, but with the young girls in the lower grade, whom I can't stand. And that's the best-case situa-tion, because my parents already told me that they don't have any more money to keep paying for the Scuola Italiana. They're tired of making so many sacrifices. They told me that if I get held back, they would send me to a technical school or to the Cu-linary Institute, and I'll end up as a cook in a hotel.

"In conclusion," she says between melancholy bites of a cookie, "I've decided to drop out of school right away and start working and make money to buy the things I like."

My tea tastes bitter without sugar, but I keep drinking it in silence.

I know what Laura likes: older guys, being the queen of the disco when she dances salsa, polo shirts two sizes too small so that the fabric makes her breasts even more noticeable, jeans chiseled on the curves of her hard bottom, and watching soap operas dreaming that someday she'll meet a producer who will discover her and give her a part, and she'll become famous and rich.

On the other hand, Laura doesn't give a damn about Aristotle or Shakespeare. The only scene she likes from *Hamlet* is when Polonius asks him what he's reading and he answers, "Words, words, words." For Laura, world culture is expressed in words, and words are a bad check. According to her, everybody talks too much about democracy, but we should take a look at what's happening in Chile. Her philosophy—live intensely today, because you could be killed at any moment.

Conclusion—she wants to drop out of school right away and get a job.

She stares at me as if she had lit a bomb and was now waiting for it to explode.

But I don't say a word because I'm thinking about what I'm seeing, and what I'm seeing in my mind, like on a movie screen, is what life holds for her if she drops out of school.

I shove half a cookie in my mouth and make it crunch as I chew it just so I don't have to talk. She raises her brows and asks me what I think. I know very well what I think, but I also know very well I'm nobody to start giving my opinion. Deep inside, what bothers me is knowing why Laura comes to me with her story instead of going to, for instance, Patricia Bettini.

"So you want to know my opinion?" I ask her.

"Actually no, Santos. I've already made my decision."

She takes a makeup case out of her purse and checks the corner of her mouth in the oval mirror. Then she runs her tongue over a small wound that surely stings.

"Did you tell Patricia?"

"Of course not."

"She's your close friend."

"She's my close friend, but she's pretty prudish, too."

I get up from my chair and open the window, looking out onto the terrace.

It's a few minutes after six, but it's already getting dark in Santiago. The tires of the buses squeal on the wet pavement and the whistles of the traffic cops are unable to ease the traffic congestion.

The drivers honk their horns as if it makes any difference.

I pour more tea. I wonder when Dad will come back.

"I need your help, Santos."

"What for?"

"I just found a job close to here."

"Where?"

"Across the street."

"So?"

"I can't tell my parents that I'm quitting school. I'll wear my uniform when I leave home, but I'll need your room to get changed. I have to wear something sexy. It won't take me more than five minutes."

"Look, Laura, you shouldn't drop out of school. I can help you with English and philosophy. Patricia can help you with math."

"And chemistry, and physics, and history, and visual arts?"

"I'd rather not help you with your scheme."

"Please, Santos. It's only five minutes. Only on Tuesdays and Thursdays."

"No."

"You're my best friend."

"Patricia Bettini's your best friend. Not me."

"Why don't you want to help me?"

"Just because! I don't feel like helping you!"

Laura Yáñez stands up and gives me an evil look, as if she wants to kill me. "You're a moralist, Santos."

Coming from her, that sophisticated word sounds awkward.

Because what she really wants to say is that I'm a scaredy-cat.

Or, like my old man would say, "You're not ethical, Nicomachus."

"Do whatever you want. You can use the apartment as you please. Here, you can have my father's key."

22

AFTER TRYING DIFFERENT HARMONIES, filling ash-trays with half-smoked cigarettes, sipping whiskeys sometimes straight, sometimes on the rocks, Bettini let himself fall on the keyboard—half drunk, half exhausted—and had a dream. The images had the grandeur and precision of a wide-screen movie.

On the stage of the Teatro Municipal, a chorus of about one hundred elegantly dressed men and women—the men in smoking jackets, the women in long silk dresses—await the conductor's entrance, while in the orchestra, string and brass instruments are tuned following the first violinist. This lively hubbub is accompanied by the cheerful talk of the audience sitting in the red velvet armchairs and the tinkling of bracelets of the ladies, who're looking at the box seats, where some of the prominent figures of Chilean society pose nonchalantly.

In his dream, Bettini sees himself behind the scene and concludes that his job there is to signal when the chorus and the conductor have to take their place at the stage. He perceives the nervousness in the audience's coughs and the cracks of the fans the ladies use to prevent sweat from smudging their makeup.

Little by little, the tuning of instruments comes to an end, replaced by an expectant silence. The first violinist has taken his place and looks toward the stage wings, nodding. An official from the Municipal, holding a clipboard with technical instructions, approaches Bettini and, touching his elbow, tells him, "Your turn, Maestro."

In a flash of fatal illumination, Bettini realizes that he's wearing an impeccable frock coat with an immaculate starched white dickey, and that he's holding a baton in his hand. He remembers now that he hadn't felt his throat so dry since his conversation with the minister of the interior. His feet feel heavy, as if they were made of iron, and he's unable to move until the man, kind but also compulsively professional, smiles gently at him.

But the man next to him steps over the line: he gently pushes Bettini to the proscenium, and when the musicians see him coming, they all stand up and the audience gives him an ovation.

Completely certain that the baton he's holding in his right hand is a dagger that he won't know how to use, Bettini delays his imminent cataclysm with theatrical bows to the audience. The ovation comes to an end only to start again immediately, a total and massive applause from those thousands of spectators who simultaneously have turned their faces toward the left side of the stage. Bettini's gaze follows theirs, and he thinks he's having a bad dream inside his bad dream when he sees that the person who comes to stand next to his podium to perform as a soloist is no other than Mr. Raúl Alarcón, Tiny, Little Kinky Flower.

The teeny tiny individual doesn't seem to be a victim of Bettini's fears and cheerfully holds out his hand to him. The conductor shakes it and, not knowing who, when, how, or why someone wrote this script for him, raises his arms, and with an energetic strike of his wrist pulls out from the orchestra the initial notes of the "Waltz of the *No*," opus 1, by Strauss and Kinky.

He doesn't understand anything, but he shakes the baton as if he were conducting Beethoven's Fifth Symphony. After a suspenseful moment, Bettini indicates with his chin for Raúl Alarcón to begin. Mr. Alarcón, exultant, proud, self-satisfied, bursts into song with the first verse of the piece he coauthored with Strauss:

We start to hear now "No, no. No, no"
all over Chile, "No, no. No, no."

In no time, a huge wave of sopranos, contraltos, baritones, basses, and tenors noisily converge in the exquisite refrain:

No, no, no, no, no, no.
No, no, no, no, no, no . . .

The sumptuous chandelier of the Municipal tinkles with the vibrations and reflects like a magic carousel the sparks of the ladies' jewels.

Bettini feels the baton starting to slip in the sweat of his hands. He feels the perspiration boiler that is soaking his starched collar, the big drops blurring his eyes.

But it's almost over.

Only one more push. Just the baritones' vibrato bringing to a closure the "no" that will give rise to the blast of the sopranos' high-pitched notes, and we're finally, at last, at the end, and the applause gets louder and louder, and Bettini knows that he must turn and bow to the audience, but he can't, he can't because something unheard of

has happened—the powerful voices of the chorus have hit and broken the theater's ceiling, and
through that hole, descending from an impeccable
turquoise sky, a rainbow of endless colors compels
him to kneel down and, in a trance, he prays to that
God that has been instantly created right there.

Bettini feels that he's being hugged and shaken.

He opens his eyes and, behind the multicolored
curtain in the last scene of this dream, he sees his
wife accompanied by Olwyn, who's pointing a finger at him.

"Bettini, I'm here with the tailor who's going to
manufacture the T-shirts for the *No*, the visual art-
ist who's going to design the flags for the *No*, the
graphic specialist who's going to print the poster for
the *No*, and the filmmaker who's going to film the
image of the *No* for our TV spot. Bettini! Do you
have the campaign logo ready for me?"

The ad agent extends his arm to the highest
black key on the piano, presses it, and, with the
pedal, keeps it vibrating in the air.

"A rainbow," he mutters.

"Bettini?"

"A rainbow. The logo of the *No* campaign is a
rainbow."

Olwyn shares his silent bafflement with the creative team and then fixes his gaze on Magdalena.

She shrugs and Olwyn points reproachfully at the half-full glass of whiskey on the piano.

"A rainbow, Bettini?"

"A rainbow, Senator."

"Don Adrián, this is a political campaign, not a carnival. It's true that the American flag has funny-looking little stars, but . . . a rainbow! I've never seen anything like that."

"Well, then, now you'll see it."

"You were recommended as the best ad agent in the country, Bettini. Don't let me down."

Suddenly Adrián seems to be coming out of his trance. He feels it in the rhythm of his new response. That staccato with which he used to dazzle clients in the good old days.

"Listen, Senator. The rainbow meets the conditions we need. It has all the colors, but it's only one thing. It represents all the political parties that are for the *No*, and no one loses its individuality. It's something beautiful that appears after a storm, and all those colors have exactly what you wanted, Mr. Olwyn—joy!"

The political opposition's leader experiences a moment of intense doubt—he doesn't know whether to surrender to the fear that threatens to overtake him or to the slight hope that is now bringing a smile to his face.

He snaps his fingers and addresses his team: "Gentlemen, the logo of the *No* campaign is the rainbow. Print it on the T-shirts, the flags, the posters, the avenues, the walls, and the sky!"

Then, with more willpower than faith, he pounces on the ad agent and wraps him in a hug.

"Was it hard, Bettini, to come up with such a brilliant idea?"

The man looks with a certain melancholy at the glass of whiskey, and bringing his lips closer to the former senator's face, whispers in his ear, "*Nocte dieque incubando.*"

"What's that, man?"

"Latin. Religious school, Senator."

"And what does it mean?"

"Thinking about it day and night."

23

PROFESSOR PAREDES comes in late to class with his raincoat all wet. He carries a paper bag with mortadella, bread, and a bottle of mineral water. He hasn't had lunch. He says that he's late because in a private school in the province there's an English teacher who's undergoing chemotherapy and he's substituting for him, so that his colleague could keep getting paid. All six feet of Paredes are full of solidarity. On Mondays he has to spend half the day on a bus to go to Rancagua and come back. He spends part of his own salary on transportation, but at least he prevents the teacher's family from dying of hunger while he applies for a subsidy from the Teachers' Union for his sick colleague. What he doesn't mention is something we all know—that the president of the Teachers' Union is in jail.

Meanwhile, Professor Paredes hurries to do his own things. He already got the plane tickets to go to the filming in Portugal, and he doesn't want to leave the play we have been rehearsing half done. So one day next week, at noon, we'll have the dress rehearsal, something that will make us, the actors, appear as heroes, because all the students will be allowed to skip class to attend the performance. And skipping classes is what we like the most at school. The brats don't know squat about theater, but they'll pack the auditorium just to free themselves from physics or chemistry.

The play's Cervantes's short farce *The Cave of Salamanca*. It's a funny story in which a husband says good-bye to his wife to attend his sister's wedding in another town. As soon as the man leaves, the lady of the house and her maid get ready for an orgy with their lovers—the barber and the sacristan of the village.

Well, I play the sacristan.

The wardrobe stylist has brought me a purple robe and some medallions to hang from my neck. When we're in the height of the feast with the maid and the wife, the husband comes back. So a guest who had arrived earlier to the house, a student from Salamanca, makes the scorned husband believe that barber and I are ghosts. The cuckholded man is satisfied with the magic from Salamanca, and we all end up happily toasting like good friends. The principal, the entire school faculty, and Lieutenant Bruna, who's in charge of our school, will all attend the premiere. Lieutenant Bruna's a big supporter of students participating in extracurricular dramatic and literary activities so that they stay away from political turmoil.

Lieutenant Bruna doesn't know that, when the school's security guard leaves, he gives us the keys, and our rehearsals of *The Cave of Salamanca* come to an end. Then two professional actors come in to rehearse with Professor Paredes a very "daring" play by Tato Pavlovsky called *Mr. Galíndez*. That's a whole different thing. The play's about two torturers who, while waiting for their next political victims, torture two whores sent to them by their boss, Mr. Galíndez.

Che Barrios brought Pavlovsky's play hidden inside a copy of *Treasure Island*.

Because of these kinds of things, my old man thinks that his colleague Paredes should take his vacation in Portugal immediately. Even though *Mr. Galíndez* will be performed clandestinely and only in underground theaters, there are snitches everywhere who may rat on him.

Several actors have received death threats. Last week, the very popular actor Julio Junger celebrated his birthday, and a messenger arrived at his place with a gift for him—a funeral wreath. Junger and Professor Paredes acted together a few years ago in Harold Pinter's *The Caretaker.*

I'm safe playing the cunning sacristan. But you never know, because last week the minister of education banned a play by Plautus written two thousand years ago. He said it was blasphemous. Of course, the title of the play was *The Braggart Soldier.* It seems that Pinochet took it personally.

I'd rather be in *Mr. Galíndez* than *The Cave of Salamanca*, but my father would die three times over if he ever found out. Besides, there are two big shots playing in it, two actors who're not allowed to perform in soap operas. Here the entire TV network belongs to Pinochet. Anyone who admits to not being a supporter of Pinochet is shown handcuffed and is accused of being a terrorist.

Patricia Bettini wants to leave the country as soon as she graduates from high school. She says that this country's hopeless. I would leave, too, but I can't leave my old man alone.

He doesn't have anyone else to take care of him. I miss him a lot.

It seems as if nothing is changing and Chile is going to rot with Pinochet. A couple of months ago they laid an ambush for him. The car he travels in was shot at. But of course nothing happened to him; the bullets shattered against the bulletproof windows. That night, Pinochet was on TV show-ing how the bullets had damaged the windows. He said it was a miracle that he was alive—indeed, the bullets' impact had drawn the face of the Virgin Mary on the glass. It wouldn't be a surprise if he now asked the pope to canonize him.

That shooting made the military very nervous. In retaliation, they immediately went out into the streets to kill people. I don't think that my dad had anything to do with that. He's a pacifist. He says that violence only brings more violence. But I'm not sure. Everything I've studied at school shows that history progresses through acts of violence—the revolt of the slaves, the French Revolution, the world war against the Nazis. But Chile is so small!

Who cares about what happens to us?

If Patricia Bettini leaves Chile, I'll lose any will to live. She studies at the Scuola Italiana, and I study at the Nacional. We share Professor Paredes.

He teaches English in both schools and directs plays in both places. Here, Cervantes (and Pavlov-sky in parentheses), and there, Ionesco.

With me he directs Cervantes. With Patricia Bettini, Ionesco.

She has an Italian grandfather in Florence. She doesn't have any problem understanding Italian movies. She can watch them without reading the subtitles.

She sings Modugno's songs and knows a Leopardi poem by heart— "Fratelli, a un tempo stesso, / Amore e morte ingenero la sorte" (Children of Fate, in the same breath / Created were they, Love and Death).

I get goose bumps, because that happens so often! We study *Romeo and Juliet* with Professor Paredes, and it's exactly the same.

Actually, it would be better if Patricia left for Italy. She wants to do something for my father. Who knows the mess she can get into. But if she leaves, I'll slit my wrists.

Nicomachus in Verona.

24

THE CAST OF VOLUNTEERS that Magdalena brings together as the producer of the TV campaign for the *No* includes the following specimens whom Adrián Bettini—not yet used to the hustle and bustle of the eccentricities created by Alarcón, the *angelorum*— watches with fear.

A bearded university student stands in front of him and asks Bettini to pose a question to him.

"What kind of question?"

"Ask me what I would say to a dictator."

"Okay," Bettini says. "Sir, what would you say to a dictator?"

The young man looks to the right, then to the left, and to the front, and then sticks out a huge tongue with a drawing of a rainbow on it, and on top of it, the word *No*. Then the man anxiously awaits for the ad agent's reaction.

"It's fine," Bettini says, meaning something else.

Actually, he wanted to say that he was sliding into a pit of nonsense, as if the whole country were using a drug that was unresponsive to any antidote.

"If you allow me to make a suggestion," the bearded man says, "I'd recommend that when I stick out my tongue with the *No*, you play the sound of a lion's roar."

"Okay," Bettini says, trying to understand why everything seems wrong.

Then Magdalena asks the second candidate to appear on the TV campaign to come in.

This time, it's a firefighter.

In a firefighter suit.

And a firefighter helmet.

He says hello to Bettini by gently striking his forehead, and solemnly says, "We, Chile's firefighters, are for the *No*."

Unable to think of anything more sophisticated, Bettini asks the man in what way he thinks a firefighter could be of help to the *No* campaign. The man gets a glass of water from behind him, raises it as if to toast and, imitating the sound of the siren of a fire engine, sings, "No, no, no, no, no, no, no, nooooooooooooo."

When he finishes, he smiles and takes a sip of water from the glass he's still holding in his hand.

Bettini hasn't had even a drop of alcohol in the entire day, but he feels as if he were drunk. He walks to the wall at the back of the set, and there he sees his daughter's boyfriend, Nico Santos, the instigator of all this, trying to memorize some lines from a book.

"Are you volunteering to appear on the TV ad, too?"

"No, Don Adrián. I'm studying for Professor Paredes's test on Shakespeare."

"And what are you reading?"

"*Macbeth*."

"Have you memorized any part of it?"

"I have."

"Let me see."

Instead of standing up to recite, the young man lies down on a blue mat and, with his chin resting on his left hand, lets Macbeth's speech flow:

Blood hath been shed ere now, i' the olden time,
Ere humane statute purged the gentle weal.
Ay, and since too, murders have been perform'd
Too terrible for the ear.
The times have been,
That, when the brains were out, the man would die,

And there an end.
But now they rise again,
With twenty mortal murders on their crowns,
And push us from our stools.
This is more strange
Than such a murder is.

"I'm confident that Professor Paredes will give me a B now," Nico Santos says, trying to hide a yawn. "What are you thinking about, Don Adrián?"

Bettini rubs his eyes and strongly presses the bridge of his nose with his fingers. "About reality. Where's reality, Nico? In Shakespeare, or in all those fools there on the set?"

Nico Santos stands up, looking at the other side of the studio, where he sees a group of girls in leotards, carrying a rainbow made of papier-mâché.

25

LAST NIGHT we went to a Prisioneros concert. Well, it was not exactly a concert. It was a "toccata." When a rock band plays, they call it "toccata." Except that the one last night was "toccata and fugue,"* because as soon as we left the premises in Matucana, we saw several vans parked at the door and the cops waiting for us.

At the beginning they were not taking anyone, but this fool shouted at the cops, "Fuck you and your horse!" So the cops took out their clubs and started to hit us on the head. We had to run. The owners of the nearby bars, as soon as they saw the cops coming, closed the metal gates, and it was impossible for us to find a place to hide.

---

* *Fuga* in Spanish is a musical form, but it also means "flight" or "escape."

Los Prisioneros' lyrics are "daring." But the country is not as daring as their lyrics. That's what's cool about rock. It's as if the songs were more alive than the people. It's as if the drums and the guitars electrified our veins. It makes you want to leave the toccata and go throw stones at La Moneda. But the truth is that the following day we're all walking with our heads hanging down, sleepy, trying to read the history chapter in the last minutes before the quiz.

And the teachers teach their classes apathetically, looking at their watches every few minutes, to see how long they have before the bell rings. They're so poorly paid! In Chile, teachers are despised. Tell me about it—my dad is a teacher.

My favorite song by Los Prisioneros is

The world needs Latin blood,
red furious and young.
Good-bye barriers! Good-bye seventies!
Here comes the strength the voice of the
*   eighties.*

Patricia Bettini listens to her old man's records, like the Beatles and that stuff. She also knows some of Joan Baez's and Bob Dylan's songs. She says that it's one thing to sing that the strength of the eighties is coming, and another for it to actually ever come. She doesn't think that rock can over-throw Pinochet. However, her national anthem is John Lennon's "Imagine," the most pacifist song of all. She thinks that there's no way to get rid of Pi-nochet, so once she finishes high school, she's leav-ing for Florence.

I shake when I think about it. Italians are so handsome, they dress like princes, get million-dollar haircuts, and play soccer like gods. As for myself, she says that if I love her, I better start learning Italian.

It sounds similar to Spanish, but that can be pretty deceiving. She gave me a couple of books, and I underline whatever I understand and like. For example, that cool quotation from Dante: "Lib-ertà va cercando, ch'è sì cara, come sa chi per lei vita rifiuta" (He is looking for that freedom so cher-ished, that for which he even despises life).

Professor Santos would wash out my mouth with soap if he heard me saying something like that. He's the only one who can be a hero in this house. He doesn't want me to be involved in anything. The other day I learned by heart some verses from a song with which I left Patricia Bettini stoned a few days ago, "Tu sei per me la più bella del mondo" (To me you are the most beautiful girl in the world).

After school, she was waiting for me. As soon as she saw me, she asked me to hug her, as tightly as

I could, and said that she wanted to die. I dropped my backpack and squeezed her behind the hot dog stand, because everybody was looking at us. She couldn't stop trembling and her cheeks were burning. I took her to the Indianápolis's ladies' room and I splashed cold water on her face.

She had come running from school.

When she arrived that morning, a helicopter was hovering over Apoquindo, and before going to class, she saw a couple of cars without license plates parked near the corner.

It's not strange that she had considered that to be strange, because in Chile we learn to pay attention to things like these, even if we don't realize it.

Just as she's entering the building, she bumps into Professor Paredes. But as she's greeting him with a kiss, as she always does, three cops come storming out of a car, grab him, drag him, and throw him into the car. The school principal starts fighting with the guys, but they hit him, throw him on the ground, abduct Professor Paredes, and flee with him in the car.

Since then, she hasn't stopped trembling.

The police came and she told them everything she had seen, about the car without license plates, while the principal is bleeding on the ground. Soon after that, the Italian consul arrived in an official car. Quickly, he got out of the car and told all the students to go into the school building.

Dante.

Freedom.

I don't know how, but while I'm hugging her so that she stops trembling, I start trembling, too.

26

SCREENING NO. 1.

Bettini talked the Argentine ambassador into inviting the leaders of the Chilean opposition to attend an homage to the great film director Armando Bo and his favorite actress, Isabel Sarli. A limited number of invitations were sent for the screening of *Flesh*, which would be followed by a tasting of pinot noirs from Mendoza and the launching of a new cabernet sauvignon produced by a Chilean entrepreneur with vineyards in Pirque, whom bankers affectionately called Vial the Democrat.

Bettini wanted the political leaders of the coalition against Pinochet to be there in order to sanctify, once and for all, the TV spot that had caused him so much distress. The attendance of these skillful leaders would give the meeting a businesslike atmosphere, which would be very helpful, since the film to be shown would actually be the first images of the *No* campaign, not the erotic story starring Sarli—that innocent creature who wonders in the film what is it in her that awakens the lust and savagery of men.

The ambassador, instead of saying "*È arrivato Zampanò*," as Giulietta Masina introduced Anthony Quinn in *La Strada*, greeted his guests with a conspiratorial "*È arrivato il No.*"

Olwyn didn't want to go to the premiere of the *No* campaign because he knew he was being watched, and he was trying to move around without being noticed. Going to the embassy ran the risk of revealing the mysteries of the *No* campaign to his rivals. The leaders of the parties didn't go either—only second-rank representatives attended.

Olwyn's absence could lead to disaster for Bettini. If the man who had asked for "joy" didn't show up, how would he explain to all those brave and long-suffering leftist activists who were ready to test him, for example, Little Kinky Flower's "Waltz of the *No*"?

Would they understand the strategy of diluting the hemlock with syrup?

He'd rather watch the first fifteen minutes of the campaign with them, just in case he had missed any details. He wanted to make sure that there were no silly images out of context that would jeopardize the broadcasting of the TV ad.

It was necessary to be careful. To denounce without provoking. And even to praise Pinochet, if it were necessary, for the courage of wanting to look like a democratic ruler in the eyes of the entire world. He was going to react right away, even before the censors, to anything that could be perceived as impertinence, so that his reputation remained unharmed.

That's why he had suggested that the ambassador invite Olwyn to watch the movie. *Impeccable*, he thought.

The minister of the interior's spies would report that Olwyn had gone to a cultural event at the embassy of the kindred country. He never expected the diplomat to really have a copy of *Flesh*.

"You're a perfectionist, Ambassador. I'm sure that when you attend a baptism you demand to see a baby, and if you attend a funeral, you get angry if there isn't a corpse around."

Bettini himself had provided Olwyn's stern emissaries with the most comfortable armchairs in an improvised first row. The ambassador lit Dutch Tiparillo cigars for them, Patricia brought some footrests so that they could stretch their legs, and Raúl Alarcón, aka Little Kinky Flower, bowed emphatically as he walked by them.

Che Barrios connected the speakers and then Bettini held out his hand, indicating that the young man should sit next to him. He wanted to have the privilege of watching his own work with the young and improvised technician sitting nearby, just in case it became necessary to interrupt the showing.

The ambassador offered some introductory words before the film. He said he was expecting to be pleasantly surprised by such an illustrious group of artists. He had to tell the distinguished friends in the audience that the minister of the interior had called him on Monday to assure him that all diplomats accredited in Chile could be certain— and to let their respective countries know—that whatever the outcome of the plebiscite, he would recommend that General Pinochet respect the people's verdict.

"That being said," the ambassador continued, apologizing in advance for the vulgar remark he would quote literally, and showing a smile with perfect teeth, "he also said to me, 'When you lose, you have to recognize that you're in the shit.'"

The ambassador to the neighboring country ended his remarks to this "ecumenical" event— smiling once again at finding such a felicitous adjective—where the leaders of the opposition parties would watch Isabel Sarli's fifteen-minute ad campaign, which would be broadcast in a few days, in the presence of their own creators.

"Although the Constitution of 1980 requires Pinochet to call this plebiscite, it's also true that the military forces have the power to put any constitution you know where when they feel like it. So let's not see things so black and white all the time, you know? The general keeps his promises, you know?"

He pointed at Bettini with his cigar and kept it in that position as he went on with his speech.

"To tell the truth, I'm afraid we'll now see something terrific, because we all know the résumé of this talented ad agent. A man who's 'a bit bitter, like life,' a man who was asked, not long ago, by the minister of the interior himself to lead the advertising campaign for the *Yes*. He, who defines himself as a David among Goliaths, has chosen, in spite of the many risks involved, to be the president's adversary. That's his legitimate right. I can't wait to see what he has invented to overthrow the general from the Chileans' heart."

The ambassador held the video of *Flesh* in one hand and the tape of the *No* in the other, and, leaning over to the delegates of the political parties, asked if he could dispense with Isabel Sarli in spite of "the two powerful reasons she'd have to occupy the screen."

They all laughed willingly, and Héctor Barrios, the young Chilean student recently repatriated from Argentina, pressed the Play button. The ambassador dimmed the lights, and the fifteen-minute campaign for the *No* began.

27

SCREENING NO. 2.

The young Nico Santos couldn't attend the private premiere of the *No* campaign. It was opening night of *The Cave of Salamanca* at his school's auditorium.

The first row was reserved for special guests—the principal and the military official in charge of the school, Lieutenant Bruna, who encouraged cultural activities as an antidote against the political protest the students were so inclined to.

Dressed for his role as the sybaritic, lecherous sacristan, Nico stepped out from behind the curtain. With a ballet-style bow, he acknowledged the applause and cheers of his friends in the audience and, asking for time out, the way basketball coaches do, he cleared his throat. He knew that he was about to violate the pact he had with his father about not getting into trouble. He missed his dad a lot, but at least he had the consolation that his father would never know about the blunder he was about to make. If Professor Santos were in the audience, he would surely intuit what Nico was about to say, and he would place his finger to his lips, urging his son to keep silent.

"You must be wondering, respectable audience, what I'm doing here dressed as a sacristan . . ."

"Yes!" the students roared.

"I'm a character from Cervantes's play *The Cave of Salamanca.*"

"Bad cave, bad luck,"* a funny one shouted from the last row.

The burst of laughter filled the auditorium. And Nico, in an accommodating mood, decided to join the racket without losing sight of his goal.

"I hope you have fun with this little piece by Cervantes. You know Cervantes, right?"

Lieutenant Bruna nodded, satisfied. "*Don Quixote,*" the official said loudly.

"The author of *Don Quixote of La Mancha,*" confirmed Nico, crediting the lieutenant with a smile for his precise info. "This is a brief piece that I hope you like. We had scheduled its premiere

---

* "Mala cueva" (literally *bad cave*) means *bad luck* in Chilean slang.

for next week, but considering the distressing circumstances surrounding Professor Paredes, the director of this play, we have decided to bring the premiere forward as a way to call the attention of all of you, comrades and school authorities, to the abduction of Professor Paredes, who, as of today, is a"—Nico swallowed—"'missing detainee.'"

All the teachers who had escorted the principal and the lieutenant to the honor row simultaneously lost their smiles. The expression "missing detainee" was taboo. The most you could say was "missing," and you had to immediately add, as in the news, "in unknown circumstances."

Nico Santos had just lighted a bomb fuse. All the students looked toward the exit door, wishing they were somewhere else.

The principal snapped his fingers and made a signal to Nico to raise the curtain.

"Let the show begin," he said as cheerfully as he could.

But Nico Santos stayed restless on the proscenium, possessed by a sudden recklessness that clouded his brain and loosened his tongue.

"I'm especially addressing you, Lieutenant Bruna, to ask you to make the most of your high rank and influence on the military forces, and to act accordingly, so that we can have our dear English teacher and director of this play back with us."

Bruna nodded with a crisp movement of his chin. "We'll do all we can."

For ten seconds, Santos and the lieutenant looked at each other amid the overwhelming silence that filled the room. Until the beautiful teenager from High School 1 for girls, who played the role of the wife, dressed in such a way that the lubricous young audience wouldn't miss the volume of her breasts, broke onto the stage caressing her husband, while crying false tears whose hypocrisy she underscored by pointing at them with a finger as they flowed down her cheek.

As soon as her husband, and future cuckold, comes onto the stage, she makes the obscene gesture with her finger upward and shouts, "Go down, lightning, to the house of that whore, Ana Díaz. May you go and never come back, like smoke."

From offstage, Nico Santos watches Lieutenant Bruna, in the first row, with his right leg crossed over his left leg, impatiently jiggling his right foot. Nico Santos lifts up the skirt of his purple sacristan gown to wipe the sweat off his forehead.

28

BETTINI'S FAVORITE LINE was by Camus: "Everything I know about morality and the duty of man I owe to soccer." Especially, he added, that the ball never comes where one expects it to.

The bitter-faced man chosen by the parties' delegates to be the spokesperson for all authorized the ambassador to put one more ice cube in his whiskey and then raised the glass to his lips.

"I think Olwyn was wrong, Bettini. You're not the best anymore. You used to be the best."

"Did you find the campaign that bad?"

"As harmless as a mint tea. That supposedly ironic parade of commanders, with Strauss's little waltz as background music, makes even the military look nice."

"Does it mean that you're not going to approve it?"

"A little waltz by Strauss! We don't have any time to change anything. We're screwed!"

"'A little waltz by Strauss,'" Bettini repeated while rubbing the glass of whiskey over his forehead to sooth the heat.

"I was expecting Troy to burn—you attacking Pinochet with the issue of the missing detainees, human rights, torture, exile, layoffs . . . And you come up with a little joke here, a little joke there . . . Strauss's little waltz! Tell me, Bettini—"

"Mr. . . . ?"

"Cifuentes. When, exactly, did you lose your way?"

"I really don't know. I've been unemployed for so many years!"

"Pinochet may win the plebiscite just because he has balls. Instead, you seem to have only songs."

The ad agent mumbled something so softly that Cifuentes had to lean forward to hear him.

"What did you say, Bettini?"

"Songs and broken collarbones."

"Don't talk rubbish, man!"

The ambassador hugged them both and walked them to the balcony. On Vicuña Mackenna Avenue, the traffic was moving very slowly.

"What a disaster!" the ambassador said. "It seems there are only red lights on this street!"

29

I TEAR OUT the calendar page. This month is full of holidays. Independence Day, Coup d'État Day, Army Day. I heard on the radio that, for this month of national holidays, there will be an amnesty for political prisoners. Maybe they'll let my dad go.

We're approaching the plebiscite.

Patricia's father changes offices every three days. He's trying to prevent the cops from breaking into the premises where he keeps the videotape with the campaign against Pinochet. He wants the images to be a secret, so the ad agents for the *Yes* don't have a chance to react.

We're in art class. The teacher just explained Van Gogh's yellow sunflowers. She says that colors elicit certain sensations and moods. Blue is the saddest of all. It's a cold color, like green. The other ones are warm colors. We are working in silence on our watercolors, trying to paint something that would evoke an emotion. On the back of the page we have to write what we expect to convey with our drawing. I peek at Che's work. It's a mountain range, but instead of painting snow on the peaks he has drawn angels shaking their wings. I don't know what he means by that.

I cannot get lost. On the back, I wrote "Joy," and on the front I drew a rainbow.

Inspector Pavez walks in. We've been instructed to stand up every time a guest enters, but the inspector makes a gesture for us to stay seated. Something in the direction of his gaze tells me that I shouldn't sit. And I'm right, because he says, in his hoarse voice, "Santos."

I know what all my classmates are thinking. I know they remember the day my father was taken. And I know they know that they're going to take me now. Daddy was right. I shouldn't have gotten myself in trouble. It was stupid to say my little speech in front of Lieutenant Bruna. The inspector puts on a serious face. Serious like a funeral. Now I'm afraid they have found my father. I'm afraid they found him dead, and that's what the principal's going to tell me. That's why Pavez has that expression on his face and is clenching his teeth.

All of the students have sat down, except Che.

"I'm going with you," he says.

He patted my shoulder and squeezed my arm.
My throat is dry.

I look at our drawings on the desks and don't
know whether or not to pack all my stuff before
leaving. Everything's happening incredibly slowly—
I don't want to leave and it seems like Inspector
Pavez wants to delay the moment he has to take me
to the principal's office.

"What's the matter, Inspector?" the art teacher
asks softly.

Without answering, the man urges me to go
with him and hurry up. I decide to leave everything
where it is.

"Che, why did you put angels instead of snow?"
I ask him, letting go of his embrace.

"We need fools."

He leafs through his sketchbook, and on most
of the pages he has drawn an angel. Sometimes flying, sometimes lying down, or sitting by the curb,
or carrying a hen in its hands.

30

AS HE WAS getting in the car, carrying the video for the first broadcast of the *No* campaign, Bettini doubted that he would be able to coordinate his movements. The extra drinks couldn't quiet the tremors running through his body. So the political delegates had found his campaign harmless, a cute footnote, too Goody Two-shoes, a watery herbal tea for an old lady.

All those nights of insomnia and fury, seated at the piano, trying to convey some "joy," have led only to the ironic smiles of the men who had hired him.

His archenemy, the minister of the interior, had achieved his purpose by getting his men to break Bettinis's collarbone, but his own clients had broken his soul.

He felt a cry in his stomach. His eyes were swollen. The drizzle was the faithful dog accompanying the beggars. He felt sorry for himself. He embraced his self-pity.

This *No*, which was supposed to reunite him with his creativity, was starting to be a farewell letter.

His father had taught him not to put too much hope in anything, not to have his present life depend on the eventual outcome of any enterprise. "Always think you're going to lose." A philosophy very different from the one practiced by his wife, Magdalena, and her friends: recommendations to improve digestion, self-help, Buddhism in daily life, Zen here, Zen there. Bad thoughts will result in bad deeds. If you think positive, happiness will come to you, wagging its little tail. He had believed in the fucking *No* with the same faith as in his childhood he had believed in a guardian angel. He had put his protection and anxieties in his hands. He had gone against his best judgment. He was sure that, this time, David wouldn't defeat Goliath. Poetry's breath like a canary wouldn't be strong enough to beat the ogre.

Magdalena's poetry ideas were sheer wishful thinking. The dictatorship's heavy sea had thrown over the rocks and beaches only debris from shipwrecks. Raúl Alarcón and Strauss, his partner; Olwyn, so convinced that he could become the king of freedom; and his own dream, that rainbow coming off the sky, were all the premonition of a cataclysm rather than a hymn to victory.

He put the key in the ignition and felt that the exhaust gas was filling the interior of the car through one of the many holes in its body. The smell of Santiago was there, an unidentifiable little animal multiplying itself in the drizzle, encouraged by the lights of the cars that moved slowly during rush hour.

Spring would be coming, but not the poet's spring. The damn spring of the radio song.

The spring of those military men who had overthrown the democratic government on a Tuesday, September 11, who now, with the plebiscite, would see the red stains magically vanish from their uniforms. Pinochet would win comfortably and would continue terrorizing the country, unharmed, dying of laughter. His generals would once again toast one another with bubbling champagne.

And people would point their fingers at him.

Like in Frost's poem, Adrián Bettini had taken the road less traveled, the road leading to originality, but also to the abyss.

His campaign for the *No* and for joy didn't interest anyone.

The minister of the interior was going to authorize broadcasting the TV ad, thanks to the harmless chorus of the Nobel Prize winner to be,

Raúl Alarcón. That little waltz had watered down the explosive fuse everyone was expecting to see in those brief fifteen minutes. Naïve humor in a country that had shed so much blood trying to earn its freedom!

Harmless.

He got to the corner and, instinctively, covered his nose for a sneeze. That second was enough for his car to crash into the vehicle in front of him. It wasn't a big deal, only one more wound on the old Fiat, one more scratch in his life, nothing compared to the huge dent in his soul.

He went from that fatalistic resignation to blind panic as saw that the vehicle he had rear-ended was a patrol van.

In a flash of lucidity, he hid the tape with the *No* campaign under the driver's seat and resignedly rolled down his window.

The honks of the other drivers, impatient with this new delay, amplified through the open window. They made his nerves screech, precisely at that moment when he needed peace, good judgment, sagacity. Mettle. Good mood.

There he was, the police officer with his excess of formality, asking him for his "documents."

He put his hand into his pocket and the invitation to the cultural event at the Argentine embassy came out along with his wallet. Perhaps the invitation would provide a rationale for softening the blow that would soon come.

Bettini handed him the invitation with the coat of arms of the trans-Andean country. After looking at it with indifference, the cop gave it back to him.

"Your documents, sir."

"Sure, sure, Lieutenant," Bettini said, digging inside his wallet. As he did this, he added, as if he were presenting an absurd safe-conduct, "I'm coming from a reception at the Argentine embassy. Right here. On Vicuña Mackenna. A reception hosted by the ambassador himself."

The officer took the documents, protecting them from the rain with his left hand.

"Your name is Adrián Bettini?"

"Yes, Lieutenant. I'm coming from a reception at the Argentine embassy. The embassy of the Argentine Republic, our neighboring country."

"Turn off the car and get out."

"Gladly, Lieutenant. I don't understand how this happened. It's a regrettable accident. The wet road, probably . . ."

"The road is wet for everyone. Only you crashed."

"You're right, Officer. Probably because I was coming from a reception at the Argentine embassy—"

"Did you drink?"

Absurdly, he tried to cover up the smell of alcohol on his breath. Equally absurdly, he replied, "I don't think so."

"You'll have to come with me to the police station, sir."

Another cop detoured the traffic to the opposite side of the road and signaled Bettini to park near the sidewalk.

"This guy's going in. Driving under the influence and damaging a vehicle of the armed forces."

Bettini parked his car near an oriental banana tree, got out, and closed the door. He was about to put the keys in his pocket, when one of the officers grabbed his wrist.

"I'll take the keys."

"But . . ."

"But what? Are you afraid that we will steal your car?"

He wasn't able to say *but what*.

There it was, the campaign for the *No* that was going to be broadcast in a few days, for all Chile to see. For his humiliation. For his funeral. His apocalypse.

Why say anything?

"I'm coming from a reception at the Argentine embassy . . ."

31

THE INSPECTOR DROPS ME at the principal's office as if I were a bundle he was eager to get rid of. He leaves the office without even saying good-bye. The door remains open and I can hear him going up the stairs to the second floor.

The receptionist operates the switchboard and talks to the principal. She only says one word: "Santos." With a gesture, she signals me to go in.

I walk into that place that holds only bad memories. I was there twice. Once, I was suspended for misbehaving, and it was the school's highest authority who informed me, "Come back with your legal guardian." The second time was for bad grades in chemistry.

"Sulfuric acid. Write the formula, Santos, one hundred times in your notebook." "Water, Professor! H_2O! Give me a break, Professor Guzmán!"

"I'm not expelling you only because you're Professor Santos's son."

"Never again."

"I'll study. I promise."

Today, the office seems even darker and colder than on those two occasions. The kerosene heater is off. The curtains look heavier. The oil portraits of the founding fathers who went to our school look older. Cold colors. A lot of black, and brown, and blue, and green.

The principal's sitting behind his desk and seems to be drawing something on a piece of paper. He may be filling the sheet with circles of different sizes. That's what I do sometimes. Like when I'm waiting for something.

In the leather armchair, wide, comfortable, worn-out, like scratched by a cat, is Lieutenant Bruna. He has set his kepi very carefully on his knees. With discipline.

Nobody says a word.

Nobody greets me.

I don't say a word either.

"It's cold outside," the principal says.

As if he wanted to confirm it, he walks to the window and lifts the curtain a little bit. The brief light that, for a couple of seconds, filters into the room crosses like a gust in front of the officer's face, who remains absorbed looking at the tips of his boots. I bear that long silence by rubbing my thighs.

"Yes, it's cold," the lieutenant repeats, an eternity later. "Did you bring your coat, Santos?"

They're going to take me, I think. Tears start to flood my eyes. For me. But even more than for me, for my dad. The tears don't fall.

"Santos," the lieutenant says, still looking at his boots, "life is difficult for everyone. For an officer. For a teacher. For a student, too. Do you understand?"

I understand, but I don't know what he's trying to tell me. Is he trying to tell me that he'll arrest me? My leather jacket is hanging on a hook in the classroom. My black leather jacket. Raindrops slide down over it. I like how I look in it. I like it when I'm playing with Patricia Bettini and she hits my back and it sounds like *chas*.

I hear the tip of the principal's pen scratching the piece of paper. The three of us are there, dancing to a silence. Just like when someone dies and they call for a moment of silence. A bus with a broken exhaust pipe passes by and goes away. And there's silence again. Blown up.

"I . . . ," Lieutenant Bruna begins.

He doesn't say more.

He comes to me and hugs me. Then he moves away and shows me his face. He looks sad.

Lieutenant Bruna's very sad. My knees are shaking. I want to ask what's going on, but no sounds come out of my throat.

My father, I think.

The officer blows his nose and regains his composure. He opens the door and asks the receptionist to go to the classroom and bring my jacket.

"A black one. Leather," I add.

"Black. Leather," he says as well.

Outside, there's a jeep waiting with its engine on. The driver's a soldier in combat uniform. Camouflage, like in the movies.

I zip up my jacket. I feel the cold on my chin. The jeep is a convertible. I have a history test tomorrow. I won't be able to study. My high school average is pretty low. I get by in English, philosophy, and Spanish. The art teacher likes me.

At the corner streetlight, the jeep stops. It cannot be true. There they go, Patricia Bettini and Laura Yáñez, crossing the street, arms around each other. They look happy. They know nothing about what's happening to me. I wonder if Santiago has always been this sad. I don't call them. There's no way I'll call them. They'd die if they saw me in this military jeep.

Lieutenant Bruna rubs his face. The cold hits hard.

We go up Recoleta, then take Salto, and end up in a neighborhood with vacant lots.

The jeep arrives in an area cordoned off by military vans. There are also two photographers with their credentials in plastic holders hanging around their necks. A priest is drinking coffee from a plastic cup. People are leaning against the walls of their houses, or sitting on the doorsteps. In the distance, a helicopter's propellers are in motion. The privates lift the white-and-red ribbons as they see Lieutenant Bruna coming.

He doesn't greet them. They point at a lamppost a few yards away. Cold metal. Tall. The light is off. There are many white clouds and a stripe of black turbulence here and there.

We arrive at the lamppost. With a rough gesture, a plainclothes police official with a sort of rosette on his lapel points at the thick mat that lies on the ground covering something. With a gesture of his chin, Lieutenant Bruna signals him to lift it. The officer pulls the mat fully off. It's the body of a man.

Professor Paredes.

His eyes are closed, and around his neck there're one or more sheets stained with blood.

"They slit his throat," the man with the rosette says to Lieutenant Bruna.

I'm unable to say anything. I can't breathe. I feel a flow running down my legs. I double up with pain and fall on my knees.

Lieutenant Bruna runs his hand over my hair.

"I did everything I could, my boy," I hear him saying. "You asked me for it, and God knows that I did everything I could."

32

HE FELT SOMEHOW CLOSE to the group of the "detained": a drunk man lying on a wooden bench, a student bleeding after being hit with a police club, a street vendor of unlicensed merchandise, a handcuffed union delegate.

Two hours had passed and not a single officer had begun any proceedings. Once in a while, an officer peeked in, took a look at the group, and disappeared into some back room. Jail is always like this. The feeling of an endless, unproductive time. A prelude to uncertainty. An intermission blown up by desperation. The humiliating wait. Time to imagine your loved ones worrying about your absence. The guard in uniform typing on an old Remington some report that a local judge would probably read a few months later.

The last time that he was taken prisoner, the cops wanted to teach him a good lesson. In a street demonstration against the rise of the public transportation fares, he tried to rescue a girl who was being dragged to a police van by some undercover cops.

He wasn't even participating in the march. He only followed the impulse of his heart. That's why, when questioned by the police, he couldn't give names or addresses of the rioters who had organized the protest, simply because he didn't know them.

Sometimes his damn heart made him act recklessly before his head could stop him.

On another occasion, he let his mouth run off, saying whatever he held true. Even though he knew there would be consequences. All those times it was he, only his own body, that was at stake. But now everything could result in a catastrophe that could affect a lot of people. If the images of the *No* campaign fell into the hands of the minister of the interior, he would have not only put at risk the people who had lent their faces to sing and fight against the dictator but also reveal the nature of his campaign to his rivals—the people working for the *Yes* to Pinochet, who would be now able to design an antidote and create a strategy to nullify whatever improbable advertising merits his naïve oeuvre might have.

He felt like a traitor for having had alcohol at the embassy, knowing that he'd have to carry the videotape in his car.

It was understandable, because he was nervous, irritated, insecure. He was going to show for the first time his masterpiece to the political delegates for the *No*, and he feared their verdict. He was so brutally out of practice. How the hell did he succumb, against all logic, to the vanity of assuming the temptation of . . . saving Chile? He corrected that pathetic idea. Chile hadn't been saved by the martyrs of the resistance movements, or by the disciplined activists, or by the hundreds of thousands of freedom lovers who had confronted the repression here and there. And he, the pope of all fools, had agreed to be the leader of a campaign that, instead of leading him to glory, would take him to hell.

Lacking any ideas, he had given in to the nonsense of an insignificant being such as Raúl Alarcón, with his "Waltz of the *No*."

Now his disastrous video could fall into the enemy's hands.

And the bad luck factor! He crashed. Against a police van! With only a little bit of ill will, taking a look at his criminal records, and viewing the videotape with his incendiary "Waltz of the *No*," the police could turn him in to the intelligence agents, who could apply the Antiterrorist Law to him.

The other collarbone.

Or maybe his femur.

And even that, with luck.

A higher officer came in from the street. He was clicking Bettini's car keys like castanets.

"Bettini," he called.

The ad agent stood up with his heart in his throat. Those keys, the sound of those damn keys in the key chain that his daughter, Patricia, had given him a few Christmases ago, was probably the toll of the bell heralding the assault and the knock out that would soon strike him.

"It's me, Captain," he heard himself saying, half coarse, half servile.

The man in uniform turned toward a low-ranking officer, so young he could have been of the same age as Nico Santos, his daughter's boyfriend.

"Search him."

The cop approached him. He began to frisk him, putting in a black plastic tray everything Bettini had in his pockets: his wallet, his dearest Montblanc pen, a clean handkerchief, a few hundred-peso coins, a comb with some missing teeth, several mint and lemon candies, and sheets of paper folded into quarters.

Bettini didn't recognize those papers. What were they?

When the cop put the tray in front of the captain, those pieces of paper caught his attention. He unfolded them, read the first one, apparently skipping some lines, and, after smoothing them against the twill of his uniform, gave Bettini a look full of interest.

"So we caught a big shot."

"Pardon me, Captain?"

The man in uniform dialed a number, slowly and delightedly, and while he waited for an answer, he moved the receiver away from his ear so that he could share the wait with all those present. When the call was answered, without ceasing to watch his detained, he said with a satisfied expression, "This is Captain Carrasco. I need to talk immediately to Minister Fernández. My password is R-S-C-H Carrasco Santiago."

His smile got bigger as he took a look at the second piece of paper.

"Dr. Fernández, I apologize for calling you so late at night, but I've got something here that might be of interest to you."

"What is it, Carrasco?"

"We arrested a little guy here"—he looked at Bettini, who was wiping his brow with the sleeve of his jacket—"due to a traffic violation. He's right here in front of me, quite nervous. We were proceeding with the routine control, when we found in his pocket some papers that you may want to see. That's why I took the liberty of calling you."

"Well done. Is it anything related to the Department of the Interior?"

"Shall I read what I have here, Minister?"

"Please."

The captain cleared his throat and, without much emphasis, delivered, flatly, the following lines.

It feels so good to say "no"
when the whole country asked you for that,
it feels so food to say no
when you have it in your heart.
With the rainbow in the farthest frontiers
even the deers are going to dance.
The No is exciting
and fills the insurrection
with tons of colors.
That's why, my dear, without hesitation
we'll say no, oh, oh.
So many times in life I looked for
a deeply felt word for "liberty,"
so many times I saw the wound
in my people sunken in adversity.
I never thought that destiny
would have the rhythm of a song,
but today I have no doubt,
as clear as water I see all now.

That's why, my dear, without hesitation
we'll say no.

"No," the precious jewel,
wave of my sea,
cloud of my sky,
fire that sings,
"no," my beautiful lover
of flaming eyes,
snow of my dream,
mountain range of my wine,
say no more,
we don't need any words.
Let's just say "no"
and we'll be together all along.

Captain Carrasco kept moving his jaw rhythmi-
cally as if following the cadence of the poem. Bettini
noticed that his face, which had been pale, was now
blushing. Listening to the text of his song, which
would be broadcast on the last day of the campaign,
was like listening to an execution sentence. Every
image in those stanzas seemed awful, when only
a few hours before—before *all* the disasters—they
had seemed brilliant to him, lines that Chileans of
all ages, lovers of the sea and the mountains, apoliti-
cals, the undecided, would respond to. Why had he
succumbed to his teenage daughter's poor judgment

when she tried to talk him into singing "It feels so good to say 'no'" even though he had never ever used, as all young Chileans do, the recurrent tag "d'ya feel it?" to ask if they had been understood.

D'ya feel it?

No, Adrián Bettini, holy father of the naïve, he admitted to himself. He hadn't *felt* a thing! Hearing the lyrics of his song from the mouth of a cop who was used to giving orders but who was somehow slow when it came to the pronunciation of metaphors, had sunk him in the deepest humiliation. He never imagined that hell always has one more level, deeper, and then another one, Comrade Dante, after which one can keep descending on and on, endlessly.

Carrasco was polite enough to raise the volume of the speaker even more, so that Bettini could hear "live and direct" the minister's comments to his rhymes. Then, after letting out a nonchalant laugh, the minister of the interior said, "In effect, very interesting material, Carrasco."

"From the political or the poetic point of view, Minister?"

"Both of them. Tell me, Captain, what's the name of my Neruda behind bars?"

The man in uniform covered the mouthpiece of the telephone and, lifting his chin, turned to the ad agent.

"What did you say your name was, asshole?"

"Bettini. Adrián Bettini."

"He says that his name is Adrián Bettini."

There was silence on the other end of the line, and then cheerful laughter.

"You don't say! You have Adrián Bettini himself right there!"

"Who's he, Minister?

"He's the leading person in the campaign for the *No* to Pinochet."

"Is he dangerous?"

"Not at all! With those rhymes . . . he's not messing with anybody."

"But in these papers he talks about insurrection. Shall I scare him a little?"

"No, man. Under no circumstances. Don't touch him even with a rose petal. We're in a democracy, my friend. Bettini can write all the nonsense he wants."

"But not against my general!"

"Even if it's against our general. That's democracy, Captain. A simple statistical exaggeration. Those assholes' votes count as much as ours."

"Then?"

"Give him back his stupid papers and let him go."

"And what should we do with his car? He hit the precinct van pretty hard."

"Send it to the auto repair shop on Carmen Street. They have a dent guy who works miracles."

"And the bill?"

"Mail it to the Department of the Interior, Carrasco. And tell Bettini that this one's on the house."

"Seriously, Minister?"

"Seriously, Captain."

"So I let him go? Just like that?"

"Just like that. Now, if you feel like it, make yourself happy and kick his ass."

Once he hung up, Carrasco, thoughtful, scratched his left temple. He made the car keys clink together once again and then threw them to Bettini, who caught them in the air.

"Poet, you can go."

"May I take my car?"

"Yes, take your fucking car, asshole."

"Thank you, Captain."

Bettini walked to the door and a young officer waved him off by lifting a couple fingers to his kepi.

"Eh, you!" Carrasco shouted at him suddenly. "That stuff you wrote about the *No* being your beautiful lover . . . You're a fag, aren't you?"

Bettini dropped his head between his shoulders. He didn't answer. For a second, he thought that it wouldn't have been so bad if Captain Carrasco had kicked his ass.

He fully deserved it.

33

THE FIRST CHAPTER of the *No* campaign will be broadcast tonight.

Professor Paredes's funeral will be held this morning.

On our way to the cemetery, some people come near to put flowers on the coffin. A delegation from the Scuola Italiana arrives in a yellow bus. Young girls and boys, all in their uniforms.

Walking behind the group, Patricia Bettini's carrying a wreath of chrysanthemums.

This morning, the press has reported the assassination on their front pages.

For the first time this month, it's sunny.

Our philosophy teacher, Professor Valdivieso, delivers a eulogy for Professor Paredes, remembering his pedagogical and artistic achievements.

ANTONIO SKÁRMETA

He played in *Fuenteovejuna*, *Peribáñez*, *Life Is a Dream*, *Mother Courage*, and *Macbeth*. He directed *Death of a Salesman* and *The Caretaker* by Pinter.

He doesn't say that Professor Paredes was about to present *Mr. Galíndez* by Pavlovsky.

He mentions that Don Rafael Paredes died under tragic circumstances.

He doesn't say that agents of the National Center of Intelligence slit his throat.

Today we would've had our Shakespeare test.

My copy of his *Complete Works* is all underlined.

The school chorus sings "Rest in peace. May the earth cover you with love."

Patricia keeps her head down. She shouldn't have come. Everything that hurts her, hurts me. Everything hurts me twice. There I see our teacher's widow. Doña María looks very pale. It seems that her tears have smudged the makeup they put on her. As Valdivieso speaks, she looks at the sun.

I'm supposed to be tough, but I can't.

I look at the sun along with Doña María. Valdivieso was chosen to read the eulogy because all the older teachers are devastated. All feeling like shit.

I miss Dad. At least Doña María has Professor Paredes's body, but all I have is my father's absence. No, that's not all. I also have hope.

Will I see him again, with his black tobacco and the ash falling onto his lapel?

I sniff. My father's not a missing detainee.

It couldn't be wrong, the Baroque syllogism. There were witnesses. More than thirty students in the classroom.

Logic. My dad is a genius at logic. The cops cannot deny that they arrested him. They have to give him back to me.

The phone calls I made were no use whatsoever. The men keep telling me that I have to be patient, that they're working on it. There's one called Samuel, although he told me that's not his real name. Samuel says that my father's case is priority number one. That he's doing everything he can. But Lieutenant Bruna did everything he could for Professor Paredes, too.

I've been authorized to speak on behalf of the students. Especially the actors in *The Cave of Salamanca*.

The four main characters in *Mr. Galíndez* have left their homes.

We're not going to present Cervantes's skits anymore. Nobody feels like it. On opening night we still had hopes that Don Rafael would appear. We have certainties now. And rage. And no enthusiasm.

Tonight the campaign for the *No* will be shown on TV. I'll watch it at Mr. Bettini's home. They're

ANTONIO SKÁRMETA

going to cook spaghetti alla puttanesca, Florentine
style. That is, with tons of olives and olive oil. I cannot cry now. I shouldn't be weaker than the widow.
I can't break down in front of Patricia Bettini, who
holds the wreath of chrysanthemums without raising her eyes.

Valdivieso finishes his speech. He folds his
sheets of paper. He puts them in his jacket and
makes a gesture with his left hand, asking me to
approach the podium. I'm carrying Shakespeare's
works in one hand, and in the other, an eraser that
I squeeze and release, squeeze and release. I look
at the audience. There are more than a hundred
people. Most of them are adults. Five teachers.

There are some students, too, the few who were
allowed to come by their parents. In the delegation of the Scuola Italiana there are seven young
women. A tall, slim man I've seen before in Patricia's house comes with them. He's the consul, Mr.
Magliochetti.

Everyone has a diplomat friend nowadays.

Just in case.

I have no idea who the others are. Relatives, I
suppose.

I should've brought a small bottle of water. I've
been clearing my throat for a while.

Patricia looks up. Her brown eyes. Her chest-
nut hair. John Lennon's "Imagine." John Lennon

was killed. The guy who killed him was holding a copy of Salinger's *The Catcher in the Rye*. There's only one photo of Salinger. He was a recluse.

Professor Paredes taught me a speech technique. First of all, "plant" yourself in front of the audience. With authority. Even if you're just a boy, you have to look like a giant.

Take a deep breath, hold it, and release it very slowly. Try to keep some air in the abdomen so that you don't run out of breath in the middle of a word. And before saying anything, take all the time you need to look at your audience. Not a quick look, like the quick flapping of a scared bird. Look at the audience as a whole, but also at each individual. Look them in the eyes. Don't rush and don't take too long. Avoid introductions and commonplaces. If you say, "I'll be brief," you're already unnecessarily lengthening your text. A speech is made of words and silences. Those silences, Professor Paredes said, are meaningful. Sometimes it's necessary to say words in order to hear the silence. There are different ways to be silent.

"Sometimes it's necessary to say words in order to hear the silence," I say aloud now. "There are different ways to be silent. There are ways to say something by remaining silent. And sometimes, the only way to say something is by not saying precisely what we all know should've been said.

"Dear Professor Paredes, today we were supposed to have a quiz on Shakespeare. *Hamlet*, *Julius Caesar*, and *Macbeth*. I underlined those Uncle Bill's speeches that caught my attention the most. I could've gotten a B. I'll read only one for you:

"'I have neither wit, nor words, nor worth, action, nor utterance, nor the power of speech to stir men's blood; I only speak right on. I tell you that which you yourselves do know, show you sweet Caesar's wounds, poor poor dumb mouths, and bid them speak for me. But were I Brutus, and Brutus Antony, there were an Antony would ruffle up your spirits, and put a tongue in every wound of Caesar that should move the stones of Rome to rise and mutiny.'

"I apologize for not translating it, but I don't want to go to jail."

I can't believe what I've just said.

I hadn't planned on finishing this way.

I got overexcited while reading Marcus Antonius's speech: "I'd put a tongue in every wound of Caesar that would move even the stones of Rome to rise and mutiny."

Lieutenant Bruna didn't come, but how many of those who're here today, with faces of bereavement, are agents? Look at the audience. As a whole and at each individual. They don't know I'm shaking. Just a boy. A giant.

I close the book and walk away from the mike. Silences and silences. Different kinds of silences. A final look. At Patricia Bettini. At the Italian consul. At the back of the crowd.

An old man raises a red flag over his head with both hands. Che Barrios unfurls another one tied to a stick and waves it. The art teacher raises hers. Five or six unknown adults raise their flags and let them flutter in the breeze. The principal doesn't see them. The principal pretends not to see them. Lieutenant Bruna excused himself for not coming "due to decency." There's a different kind of silence now. A silence that allows us to hear the tapping of the red flags against the air.

Only one flag is different from all the others— the flag that Patricia Bettini's raising right now. A white flag with the image of a rainbow.

34

"TOO LATE FOR ANYTHING. All the cards are dealt, Bettini. We'll show whatever you have. We'll go out fighting with our bare hands. Whatever is done, is done, even if it's total nonsense," Olwyn blurted out with a weak smile.

In accordance with the current legal resolutions, it's mandatory for all TV channels in the country to broadcast tonight the ads of the *Yes* and *No* campaigns. We wish you a calm and pleasant dinner, and a happy return to your programming.

Appetizers: tomatoes with olive oil and mozzarella cheese. *Molto* Italian, Adrián. Red cabernet wine. Main course: spaghetti alla puttanesca. With black olives, garlic, red wine tomato sauce, with capers, and onions, and pasta al dente. Not so soft that they'll stick together, nor so hard that they won't absorb the sauce.

Homemade bread, like little buns, warm and crunchy. In front of each dish, a small plate with butter.

There are four party guests. There's Valdivieso brut champagne. It's chilled, but nobody opens the bottle. Not even a thimbleful of joy comes out of this group. *What can come out of this melancholy seed?* Magdalena thinks, showing her biggest smile. Her husband, Adrián, smiles as well, and Patricia caresses her hair over and over, following a line of thinking that leads her nowhere.

No one wants to ask the other, "What are you thinking about?"

In a few minutes, the cards will be dealt, Adrián Bettini. Whatever your imagination gave birth to will be there, for all of Chile to see. Don't jump to negative conclusions. Think that there are a lot of people who will vote for the *No*. Almost half the country. Those are already persuaded. Whatever the campaign for the *Yes* or you does, they won't change their minds. Instead, your target's those who're afraid to be filmed while they're voting, who're afraid to be stabbed because of the way they vote, the undecided who fear that, if the military leaves, there will be chaos and unrest. That's why, Adrián Bettini, you have to encourage them, first to vote, then to vote for the *No*. Don't mull over the past. We all regret the past. Give us some future, some transparent air. Make them see how Chile will be without the dictator in power. Without the fear of disappearing. A country without beheadings.

"Instead of that," Bettini thinks while he passes the olive oil to Nico Santos with a gentle smile, "I have disrespected everyone. With the 'Waltz of the *No*,' I have trivialized the relevance of this historic moment. Why did I do that?"

Nico thanks him with a charming smile. Fatally wounded. And Bettini smiles back.

"You're sad, Nico."

"I am, Don Adrián."

"Then why do you smile?"

"Me? It may be because of Shakespeare."

Patricia spreads butter on a piece of bread. She thinks of the chain of associations that could cause a short circuit: Shakespeare, Mark Antony in the cemetery, a play, *Mr. Galíndez*, the dagger, Professor Paredes, her father. Nico's father, Rodrigo Santos.

"Get some wine. Shakespeare?"

"There's a character in *Romeo and Juliet*, Don Adrián, called Mercutio. He's Romeo's close friend. And one day, they're walking around the market in Verona, and Tybalt, Juliet's cousin, shows up. He's a naughty guy who's constantly provoking the Montagues. They call him the Cat, because he brags about having many lives."

"I don't remember that part. I remember the moon—'Swear not by the moon.'"

"Tybalt starts insulting Romeo and challenges him to unsheathe his sword. But, of course, Romeo's crazy about Juliet, so he's not going to start fighting to the death with his beloved's cousin. So he says to him, look, I'm sorry, but I have reasons to love you that you can't even imagine. How was Tybalt supposed to know that Romeo was dating his cousin? So when Tybalt hears all that stuff—"

"Get some wine."

Magdalena fills the glasses, but no one drinks.

"—when Tybalt hears all that touchy-feely talk about I have reasons to love you, he starts baiting Romeo, calling him bland, sissy, scaredy-cat, you know? So when Mercutio hears this, he starts calling him names, and unsheathes his sword in front of Romeo and challenges Tybalt to fight with him . . ."

"I remember that part now," Bettini says, looking out of the corner of his eye at the countdown for the campaign ads on the digital clock of Channel 13, thankful for being taken to medieval Verona at least for a while.

"And that's when everything goes to hell. Because to prevent his girlfriend's cousin and his best friend from killing each other, Romeo grabs Mercutio by his arm. And of course Tybalt takes advantage of that and, seeing him defenseless, drives his sword into Mercutio. Poor Mercutio falls to the ground, bleeding, and Tybalt and his gang split."

"Romeo might have felt real awful," Bettini comments, absentminded.

"Terrible. Then their friend Benvolio leans over Mercutio, who's bleeding from his mouth, and asks him . . . and asks him . . . how do you feel? And do you know what Mercutio says to him?"

"Tell me."

Bettini turns his back to the TV set not to see the fateful clock advancing.

"Mercutio answers him: 'The wound is not so deep as a well, nor so wide as a church door, but it's enough, it'll serve. Ask for me tomorrow and you shall find me a grave man.'"

"And that's why you were smiling?"

"That's why, Don Adrián. Imagine. The guy is on the verge of dying and he comes up with all this gibberish!"

"And you remembered that."

"And when you said . . . When you said . . ."

Nico covers his face with the napkin and suddenly bursts into tears.

Patricia looks at Magdalena, Magdalena at Adrián. Adrián takes a sip from his glass of wine.

Fucking Shakespeare, he thinks.

35

IF HE HAD BEEN ASKED about dinner, Bettini wouldn't have known what to answer. He didn't even know what he ate. His fate as a reborn ad agent was not the only thing at stake, but also the fate of the entire country. There was a small crack in the cave through which some light could come in. He feared having wasted that chance. If the whole country was shaken by violence, how could joy look believable?

And he had done the TV campaign without answering that question. Actually, sponsoring joy so blatantly, with a waltz by Strauss and a parade of lunatics saying *No* in multicolor, not having made room in his images for a single tear, knowing, as he knew, that in that precise moment Chile was crying! Everything had been a mistake.

He had given himself up to an irresponsible fiction. A desperate way out. Trying to leap into the void without a net. He explained to Olwyn that Pinochet had had total control of the media for fifteen years to impose his orders on TV screens. But he was given fifteen minutes, only fifteen minutes, a handful of seconds to break, once and for all, the relentless assault of dictatorship.

He didn't have time for subtleties. It was fifteen minutes against fifteen years. And of those fifteen minutes, almost five were dedicated to the insanities of the "Waltz of the *No*."

By dessert, Nico Santos's napkin looked like the canvas of a sunken sailboat. Bettini didn't want to comfort him. He wished he could be comforted himself. Impatience demolished him. On the screen, the images of the *Yes* campaign were flowing—hooded terrorists with bombs in their hands throwing stones at car windows: that was the joy of the *No* coming up. Chaos, the rape of teenagers, children slaughtered by a red bulldozer. The same way he was playing the card of the joy of change, Pinochet's ad agents were staging the hell of debauchery.

He didn't want to wait the few remaining minutes. Watching his images flow in front of his family would surely embarrass him. He grabbed Nico's napkin and tossed him his own. He put the wet cloth in his jacket pocket and announced to the group that he was going out for a walk.

"What are you going to do?" Patricia asked, suddenly standing up.

"Just what I said. A walk."

"But, Daddy. This is your shining moment. All of Chile is glued to the TV screens at this very moment."

"That's the problem, honey—everyone will see that their emperor is naked. I'm not in the mood for another hara-kiri."

"Dad, what are you really up to?"

"I'm taking a walk!"

Magdalena threw herself on him and challenged him to look her in the eyes. "Patricia's right. Where are you going?"

He squeezed Nico's wet napkin in his pocket.

"I won't throw myself in the Mapocho. At this time of the year, there's not even that much water . . ."

"So?"

"I'm just going to take a walk, ladies. A simple and athletic walk to breathe some fresh air."

Embarrassed, Nico stood up, and walked to the bathroom. "Excuse me."

Bettini responded with a blink of his eyes.

"You should take better care of him. Right now, he has no one to call his own."

He felt like slamming the door but decided to be gentle, closing it as if he were kissing it good-bye.

The night was cool. He buttoned his shirt's top button and looked at the moon, fractioned by the branches of the trees. He had always lived in Ñuñoa. He had the habit of feeling and admiring the old cobbled streets. The grand old trees grew without control, inhibiting the arborists with their height. There was something successfully familiar in this middle-class neighborhood. His street was far away from the supermarket, the malls, and the stops of the main bus lines.

On the corner, there was a grocery store whose owner still paid something for empty glass bottles. And when the kids went to buy bread or oil for their mothers, he still gave them a candy or a bubble gum as a bonus.

The guy from the newsstand kept the Sunday paper for him till noon, because he liked to stay in bed until lunchtime, and if he didn't go to pick it up, the guy rang his doorbell and handed him *El Mercurio* with a cheerful smile.

He had credit at the Chinese restaurant on Manuel Mott Street, and if he didn't have enough to invite Magdalena and Patricia for dinner, old Tin-Lung, laughing out loud, would write down the check amount in a huge notebook with a calendar picture of Marilyn Monroe. Everything had remained the same since his childhood, except for two details.

The TV antennas in every window, launched into the clouds.

And the Italia movie theater.

After going bankrupt, its 35-mm projector had been sold at a flea market. Those premises were now in the hands of some evangelical Christians, dressed in brown suits, white shirts, and ties, and with tons of hair gel, even in the hottest summer. Their wives, skinny, with olive faces. Some of them wearing socks up to their knees. It was still possible to see under the cobbles the tracks of the tramways that had stopped working decades ago. His neighborhood had witnessed his furtive kisses to the prettiest girl on Antonio Varas Avenue. And the day he turned fourteen, the blond girl with untidy curls who worked at the unisex hair salon allowed him to do everything on a Friday night, after closing the door behind her last customer. Then, cleaning his surprised sex with a wet towel, she whispered in his ear, "Happy birthday."

That was his Santiago. The splendor of democracy and street demonstrations. As a student, he had shouted along with thousands of citizens, "Allende, Allende, your people defend you."

In front of the police academy, on Antonio Varas, he had seen the tanks of the coup d'état, going to La Moneda. He had been awakened by the fighter planes that were going to bomb the palace.

The same week he had been obsessed with Bob Dylan's song, "Don't Think Twice, It's All Right."

So was that his style? Every historical episode came with the emotion of a particular melody, of the lines of a poem. Of course, one thing had nothing to do with the other. One was reality, and the other was fantasy. Dreams. Dissolving foam. Thin clouds.

Even though his pace was firm and energetic, he realized that his efforts were in vain. As he walked down the side roads under the smell of spring jasmines, the "Waltz of the *No*" was coming out from the windows of each one of those houses and apartments.

Paradox: he had fled that circus, and now he was overwhelmed by hundreds of TV sets.

In the vegetal darkness of the bushes, the TV screens flashed like ghostly sparks. He felt like a condemned man walking to the gallows who has to bear one more agony—to hear the music of this infamous life at a high volume.

My goodness! Oh my God, my dear God, he thought, as he started to run without any direction. *All of Santiago is watching it!*

Soon enough, sweat bathed his pale face. Although he felt his heart pumping way too fast, he didn't slow down. His heart was showing him the right way. His much desired end. Just like on New

Year's Eve when the fireworks crossed the sky, he was now having his own fanfare—the flashes from all the screens in all the Chilean homes that were witnessing his fifteen minutes of fame, his absurd and ridiculous libertarian song.

There was no need to throw himself to the Mapocho, jump from a building's terrace, hang himself from a tree, fall under the wheels of a bus.

Everything could be much neater—keep running and running until his heart exploded like a grenade.

Suddenly, the music stopped, indicating that the ad for the *No* had ended.

Now the ordeal would begin.

In that precise moment, all the inhabitants of his country, the sailors at sea, the rebellious students, the sons and grandsons of the executed and the disappeared, their mothers and girlfriends, would be puzzled, looking at each other, wondering, "What was that?"

No! "What the hell was that?"

The desired end.

His own apocalypse.

The ignominy of his entire career.

He was exhausted. When he arrived at the square, he stopped near a fountain and let the drops of water splash his face.

Suddenly, he had the feeling that all that liq-uid fogging up his glasses was giving rise to a hallucination.

There, on the other end of the square, some-thing vague was taking place.

A creature turning around giddily.

Or were there two?

The closer it came, the more real it looked. Until it became clear. Definitively true.

A young couple was turning around incessantly, as if dancing a waltz without music, as if dancing to the memory of a waltz in the starry night. As they danced, they moved freely around the empty square, and when they were so close that they could touch him, the dancing woman shouted, "We're going to win, sir. We're going to win."

Bettini took off his glasses, cleaned them with his shirttail, and, looking at the hallucination, as real and precise as it was, he told them, "No kid-ding! I'm about to have a heart attack."

36

I TAKE THE SUBWAY to go downtown.

Laura Yáñez wants to see me. She can't tell me anything on the phone. Only in person.

I've done this many times, but today there's something strange in the air. Although it's hot and the train's crowded, nobody seems annoyed. They greet each other. They move to make room for new passengers getting in.

They look carefree. There's something mischievous in their eyes. They talk. I don't see anyone with his eyes fixed on his shoes. A group of women wearing the uniforms of a supermarket are smiling, even though they're not talking to each other.

On the front page of the most popular newspaper that the retired man is reading, there are two huge pictures.

In one of them, Pinochet, smiling. In the other, Little Kinky Flower with a presidential sash across his chest.

The headline says: DUEL OF TITANS.

We're approaching the plebiscite and, from what I can hear while I move from one train car to another, nobody talks about anything else. Like a constant *tic-tac* I hear yes-no, no-yes, no-no-no, everywhere.

Santiago seems different nowadays.

Everybody looks so healthy. Did they drink some fruit juice? Did they rub themselves with seaweed in the shower? And the laughter! A red-haired high-school student with green eyes describes the scene from the night before, when the firefighter holding a glass of water imitated the siren of his fire truck, howling, "No, no, no, no, no, no, no, no, no, no." The adults smile at him. An older man gives him a pat on the shoulder. So the redhead says to him, "I could do it again if you want." And there's more laughter. It looks like a different country. Everybody says that Brazilians are this lively. "*Apesar de você amanhã há de ser outro dia.*" I feel happy for Mr. Bettini. For Patricia Bettini. For Mrs. Magdalena. When he went back home, the phone rang until three in the morning. Congratulations. Bettini was now giving interviews to foreign newspapers. He had a call from a Mr.

Chierici, from the *Corriere della Sera*. Long distance. And from another one—a Spaniard, from *El País*. They wanted his analysis and predictions for the plebiscite. The calendar is burning. How many days until October 5?

When the train arrives at a station, some passengers leave, and the ones who get on look as if they were charged with fresh batteries. Like when in the second half of a soccer game the coach sends an exhausted center forward to the bench and a substitute comes in, running a little bit to warm up. Even the train seems to be running faster. That's what my old man hates—the subjectivisms that prevent us from perceiving the objective reality. He can't stand the Sophists. Good at talking and wasting time. But deep down, it's all rubbish. Aristotle, on the contrary, he goes right to the point. Nico Santos. Short for Nicomachus.

I feel that I'm the only one in this car who's getting more and more absorbed in his own thoughts. The sadness of Dad's absence gets me down. I'm on a different frequency from the rest of the city. There'll be free elections, but my dad's in jail. In jail and missing.

That guy, Samuel, is doing as much as he can. Patricia Bettini insists that I need to talk with the bad guys. The good ones can't do anything. Now's probably a good time to do it.

Now that people seem more spirited.

Sure, I think, but I wonder how Pinochet is feeling.

Furious. He might be red with anger. It seems that it backfired on him. The lady in green who carries the bag of vegetables is humming the "Waltz of the *No*." Maybe this is just a dream and now a military commando will storm in and start shooting everyone.

I skipped school today. I'm afraid that the text I read at the cemetery will have consequences for me. Lieutenant Bruna wasn't there, "due to decency." But the snitches who were there might be waiting for me at the door of the institute.

Or sitting in my classroom.

With their short hair.

Sunny day.

They have an investigator's badge that they show by opening their jackets. They're detectives. But I was told that, afterward, the detectives hand the prisoners to the political cops.

That's when their trail is hard to follow.

The last time I talked to Samuel, he told me not to lose hope. He said that we could have good news at any time. "But also bad ones," I shouted over the phone. He remained silent for half a minute, and then he said, "Yes, but also bad ones, my boy." I apologized.

I get off at Alameda with Santa Lucía Hill and walk to Forest Park. That's where Laura Yáñez lives. She wanted to get together because she has something to tell me. I don't know what it is.

But she said that it was urgent.

It's a good idea to disappear from home and school for a while.

Laura Yáñez is so beautiful! At school, they call that kind of woman "a hell of a brunette." She told me once, "I want to be Chile's hell of a brunette." Her friendship with Patricia's based on their interest in theater. My girlfriend always looks for intellectual plays, with some political vein. She cracks up laughing with Beckett or Ionesco. Theater of the absurd. Laura's crazy about John Travolta. She knows all the dance steps in *Saturday Night Fever*. But she's never found a guy her age who could dance along with her. With her and Travolta. That's why she's always hanging around with older guys.

Sometimes, after the Scuola Italiana, Laura and Patricia go to the movies. They're so different! My beloved Bettini wants to go to Italy to visit the museums in Florence and to get to know Fellini in person. *Amarcord* drives her out of her mind. Instead, Laura . . . Laura wants to be on the cover of *Vanidades* or *Fotogramas* someday.

She'd like to play the role of femme fatale in a soap opera. But the funny thing is that she's as nice as they come. If she were rich she would be sharing everything with her friends.

She's the superfriend. But with her body, everyone wants to hook up with her.

Those dudes don't want to be just friends with her. That's why she came to me. Because she knows I'm neutralized by my love for Patricia Bettini. She knows I'm not going to cheat with her best friend.

I finally agreed to let her use my apartment so she could change. I didn't ask her anything else. I'm fucked-up enough. I don't need to start fucking up others.

And now she becomes very mysterious and tells me she wants to see me. She tells me she appreciates it but she doesn't need the apartment anymore. She wants to give me back the keys. She has her own place now, in Mosqueto, near the Palace of Fine Arts. "Come with Patricia one of these days. She likes paintings." Her parents shouldn't find out. Patricia Bettini better keep quiet. If she says something at school, and Laura's parents find out, they will kill her, literally. Anyway, by December, she'll have to tell them the truth. She hasn't been to school for a month.

I ring the doorbell. Apartment 3A. Third floor. Tiny elevator. Modern building. Only two people fit in it. Schindler. Weight should not exceed 300 pounds.

If . . .

I don't even want to think about it.

Hmm . . . If the cops are looking for me because of the speech I gave at the cemetery, I could hide in Laura Yáñez's apartment.

For reciprocity's sake.

Would she agree?

Anyway. Nothing's going to happen.

I read Uncle Bill's entire speech in English.

English. My only B. My best grade.

Because I like rock music and Don Rafael liked me. He liked that I was in the drama club. They killed him. Just like that. Lieutenant Bruna did everything he could.

What in hell, then, is "to do everything I can"?

I bring the last issue of *Caras* in my backpack. It's the kind of magazine that Laura likes. Shiny, with tons of ads, a lot of social life, and full-color fashion pages.

"You came, dude!" she says, kissing me on the left cheek and pulling me in.

"Why so much mystery?"

"I'll tell you right away. How's Patricia doing?"

I say, "Fine. Patricia's fine."

Although in fact I don't know how she's doing. I haven't asked her. Her Professor Paredes was killed, and her father has had a crushing success with his campaign for the *No*. She must be feeling terribly bad, and probably also good. Everybody's talking about the campaign for the *No*. Calls of congratulation until three in the morning. We heated up the pasta puttanesca and opened another bottle of red wine. Don Adrián gave me money for a cab. The subway wasn't running that late.

"And you?"

"I don't know, dude. But I called you because love is repaid with love."

"Where did you get that?"

"I don't know. My grandma used to say that."

"What's the matter? Here. I brought you the latest issue of *Caras*."

"Wow! With Michelle Pfeiffer on the cover! A superwoman. Isn't she?"

"She's pretty."

"Your type, right?"

"I don't know, Laura. I've just become eighteen. I don't know what my type is. And I don't understand a thing."

"But since Patricia Bettini . . ."

"What? What about her?"

"Since she's so . . ."

"So what?"

"Elegant. On the other hand, me . . ."

"You're different, Laura. No one is better than the other. You're just very different."

"Do you like me?"

"I think you're gorgeous."

"I have Coke, Bilz, Pap, and beer. Escudo beer only."

"Coke."

"With ice?"

"Three cubes."

She goes to the kitchen and brings a Coke, family size. She had prepared a small plate with cubes of cheese and green olives. It's noon, but it looks like an evening cocktail.

"Sit down or you'll fall dead tired."

"So, tell me," I say, while obeying her.

She makes herself comfortable on the edge of a wicker sofa with brown cushions. Very ladylike, she brings her knees together, not to expose her thighs, matte and smooth.

"It's about your father, Nico."

Aha. That's why she wanted me to come. No phone calls. I don't want to know about it. I want to die in advance. To die right away.

"Do you know anything?"

Laura looks at the walls of her living room and at the door leading to the bedroom, and then at the one leading to the small balcony. There's a reproduction of a painting of dancers, by Degas, and a huge photo of Travolta in a white satin suit, very tight, and an unbuttoned vest.

"Nico . . . I know how to get to him."

"Is he alive? Professor Paredes was . . ."

"I know."

Something holds her back. She wants and doesn't want to tell me. Why did she make me come?

"Please."

She shakes her shiny mop of hair, jet black and curly, and stares at me, steadily, in the eyes.

"What I'm going to tell you speaks badly of me. But I'm only going to tell you, because you gave me a hand."

"Okay. Tell me."

"I find you pretty childish, but I've always liked you. I'll do it for you. And for Professor Paredes. He gave me a D. For the first stanza of Poe's 'Annabel Lee.' Do you remember? 'Your little D,' he said to me."

"I don't get it."

She rubs her nose and sniffles as if she had a cold.

"A guy got this apartment for me. D'ya get it?"

"Yep."

"A married guy."

"Okay."

"An agent."

"From the CNI, the intelligence agency?"

"You're not that childish . . . Why? Are ya' gonna lecture me now?"

178

I don't know. I don't know what to do or say. I wasn't expecting this. I drink half the glass of Coke. I have a piece of ice in my mouth and I move it with my tongue from one side to the other.

"No, I'm not."

"I believe that, through him, we can get to your dad."

"Why?"

"I just know it, Nico."

I'd like to be an adult. To understand more about life. To have read more books. To know the psychology of people.

"What do I have to do?"

Laura leans toward me and takes my hands. She then takes them to her mouth. She doesn't kiss them. She just touches my fingers with her lips.

"D'ya have any money?"

I look at her. I look at her with all my soul poured into my awe.

"Where from, Laura? I haven't even picked up my dad's check from September. I'm terrified that they'll take me."

"D'ya know where to get a few bucks? Sell something?"

"Like what?"

"I don't know. A car."

"We don't have a car. We walk. Or take the subway."

"A TV set."

"Everybody has a TV. What are they going to give me for a TV?"

Laura separates my fingers and kisses them, one by one. Then she blinks three or four times. She doesn't look at me.

"I understand, Nico. I do."

She goes to a wood cabinet and takes out a bottle of Bacardi white rum. She pours some in my glass and a little bit in her own glass.

"Then I don't have any option, except to see how much this fucking cop loves me."

37

RAÚL ALARCÓN, Little Kinky Flower, called Adrián Bettini to thank him, enthusiastically, for having included him in the campaign. "I'm the most popular man in Chile," he said. "People kiss me in the streets. A taxi driver didn't want to charge me for the ride—'If you're brave enough to confront Pinochet, why not me? I'm going to vote *No*. And I'm going to convince everyone who takes my taxi that they should vote *No*. Great, Don Flower. Really great!'

"Thank you, Don Adrián."

"There's nothing to thank me for," Bettini said, looking through the window at a gray car without license plates parked across the street from his house. The driver lowered the window, and his companion—whose face he wasn't able to see—lit a cigarette for him. The driver half opened the door and activated the mechanism to push his seat back. He made himself comfortable and blew a puff of smoke through the window.

"Nothing to thank me for, Mr. Alarcón. I'm the one who should thank you."

"Me? But I'm nothing. A poor little kinky flower."

"People think that you're a hero. A great future is waiting for you, my friend."

The companion of the man in the gray car got out, crossed the street, walked to Bettini's door, and looked at the number. Then he compared it with the one written in his notebook and gave the driver a thumbs-up, signaling that it was *okay*.

"A great future, my friend," Bettini repeated.

He gestured Magdalena to go to the balcony and take a look at the car.

He covered the mouthpiece of the phone and whispered to her, "Go and buy something at the grocery store and take a good look at the driver's face."

"Don Adrián, do you think that we're going to win the plebiscite?"

"The plebiscite, sure," Bettini said, blowing a kiss at his wife. "But I don't know if they'll accept the outcome."

"They have no option, Don Adrián. The foreign press is here, and the reporters told me that they're going to stay until election day."

The driver's companion was now looking at Magdalena, who was crossing the street on her way to the grocery store. He put his finger just below his eye, signaling the other to pay attention.

"Tell me something, Mr. Alarcón . . ."

"At your service, Don Adrián."

"By any chance, do you have a friend with a small house outside Santiago? In the countryside, or on the coast?"

"Sure. Fernández, in Papudo. Why?"

"Well, the weather is so nice and I've seen you looking a little pale. Why don't you go to the beach for a few days, to sunbathe and rest?"

There was a long silence on the other end of the line. Then Alarcón cleared his throat and asked, "Is there anything wrong, Mr. Bettini?"

"No, nothing. Nothing."

"Excuse me for asking, but . . . are you afraid?"

"No, my friend, no," Bettini answered, while looking for the number of the Italian consul in his address book.

"Because, as for me, I can say that . . ."

"Shit scared?"

"Well . . . not as much as shit shit-scared, but . . . close. I'm sorry, Don Adrián. I didn't want to bother you. It was only to thank you . . . for having believed in me . . ."

Bettini smiled bitterly. He didn't tell him what he really had to tell him: "I didn't believe in you. I doubted you all along. Until last night, I was sure that you were a complete fool."

"Bravo for your waltz, Little Flower."

"I did nothing, Don Adrián. Strauss is the great one."

"Take care. Is everything okay at your place?"

"Everything's perfect. You know . . . People love me."

"Much deserved."

Bettini hung up and called the Italian embassy at once.

Little Kinky Flower hung up and looked again, worried, at the black car parked a little farther down the street, near the square.

38

A FEW DAYS BEFORE the elections, sociologists published the results of their polls.

Sixty-five percent of the undecided had now decided to vote *No*.

This, added to the great majority that would vote *No* regardless, the poll numbers assured that the option against Pinochet would win the plebiscite.

The team commanded by the minister of the interior didn't show any reaction or flexibility in the face of the new wave of popularity that the *No* was riding. They appeared on numerous TV programs, benefiting from the government's TV monopoly, and they never tried to address the undecided— only their own most fervent supporters.

Pinochet continued to trust Minister Fernández and his advisers, who presented him only the polls that looked favorable. The *No* campaign was harmless, and sociologists, who were giving the victory to your enemies, my general, are a gang of laid-off delinquents.

One of those laid-off delinquents had written, "The gods blind those whom they wish to destroy."

At Bettini's house, everybody's spirits had been lifted almost as much as in every Chilean province. In a country where the main entertainment was TV, the emergence of the *No* in the media lessened the loneliness that was haunting the lives of every person or family. The long-standing hopelessness was somewhat softened.

For the first time, sociologists explained to Bettini, people were feeling that TV was talking to them instead of ignoring them. Those fifteen minutes were a big bang of stellar images that didn't vanish immediately after the transmission. They kept on producing new constellations, new bursts of energy everywhere. The grave grimace had relaxed; the bitter expression on their faces had given way to smiles.

Up to that moment, what wasn't shown on the screen didn't seem real. People felt that the fictitious, banal characters on the TV shows were more real than themselves. They had only silence. They didn't have authorization to live, only to witness the lives of those unreal beings they watched every night.

That brushstroke of democracy that Pinochet had allowed had broken the dam. The strategy that seemed a harmless little game had sparked the longing for a future and happiness. Slowly, Bettini was starting to believe it, too. But his success was becoming more and more dangerous. From American films, he had inherited a word that he used only when he was among trusted friends—*fucking*. Now he was able to talk about his *fucking success* with a half smile. The days before the elections he barely slept at all. There was an excess of adrenaline around him, which didn't allow him a single moment of calm.

There were rumors that the military, aware that the eventual outcome might not favor Pinochet, were going to send all this democratic comedy to hell and not announce the results of the plebiscite. Others said that they were going to fabricate acts of terrorism to have an excuse to suspend the elections.

The parties favoring the *No* called on voters to choose *No* without hatred, violence, or fear.

On October 5, Bettini arrived at his polling station, near Egaña Square, accompanied by Magdalena and Patricia. He stood in line under a cheerful sun, buying, every once in a while, a few small bottles of mineral water from the street vendors. As he was approaching his voting table, his heart began to pump faster. That apparent routine made him feel happy. He had imagined everything more solemn and complex. But it wasn't. There he was. One among hundreds in his Ñuñoa. One among hundreds of thousands in Santiago. One among millions in Chile. Where might Little Kinky Flower be voting? Bettini was as thankful for his anonymity as the singer was happy with his popular acclaim.

If the *No* won, he vowed he wouldn't ask anything else from life. Maybe to rent a house on the beach, to take his favorite cassettes, his Greek history books. (Hmm! "The gods blind those whom they wish to destroy.")

If the *No* won . . .

Actually, he couldn't conceive a future beyond the *No*. It felt weird to think that this was only one step on the way to something bigger. This insignificance, his rainbow, his handful of images, Alarcón's waltz, deep down, they were . . . everything.

The crowning moment of his life.

Let others worry about the future. He—he raised a fist and kept it in the air when an acquaintance greeted him from the other side of the line—wanted only to enjoy the present. The eternity of this precise moment.

We only need for the *No* to win.

———

AT MIDNIGHT, he leaned out of the window just before the secretary of the interior made the results known. The commanders of the armed forces had gauged the country's climate and it was too late for them to ignore or falsify the votes.

"There are already so many people celebrating in the streets that it would be an atrocity to start shooting," the minister of the interior reported to the palace.

Undersecretary Cardemil announced that the *No* had won fifty-three percent of the votes.

The journalists, swinging between ecstasy and disbelief, looked for the minister of the interior. But they didn't find him.

Finally, Pinochet consented to talk to them. Wearing civilian clothes and overbright makeup, he delivered his verdict before dozens of cameramen from the national and international press. "One day, the Jews also had a plebiscite. They had to choose between Christ and Barabbas. And they chose Barabbas."

And he left with a smile. "No more questions."

At Bettini's house, the glasses of white and red wine were followed by a bottle of champagne, and the champagne and the phone calls were followed by a shift change at the gray car, which remained in the same place since the day it was first parked there.

It was a constant and punctual presence. A massive stillness. Sometimes there was nobody in it. At times two men got in. Sometimes the same two men who were there the first day came back. Sometimes two different guys were there. They turned on the radio, listened to rock music, then shifted to cumbias, and one day they even played Mozart's *A Little Night Music* very loud.

The car was never moved. It was always there. Permanently. Without the license plates.

The two men used to bring paper bags from the market on Irarrázabal Street. They'd peel oranges and throw the skin on the ground.

One smoked. The other didn't.

The guys in the night shift didn't smoke.

In the morning, a motorcyclist came with a thermos of coffee and sandwiches for them.

At five in the morning, Patricia came in bringing the international press wires. The Italian consul had gotten them for her. He came in with the girl, his teeth chiseled with toothpaste, his hair still wet from an early shower, a decoration on his lapel, and some Parmesan cheese and prosciutto.

He gave Patricia the honor of reading the wire from *Le Monde*. She got the meaning of the text in a few blinks and mentally translated it.

Relatives and friends had collapsed on the carpet and armchairs like exhausted warriors.

"*Le Monde*: 'There are few precedents to judge what has happened and is still happening in Chile. The most authoritarian and repressive regime in the history of the nation has become a magma of hesitation, impotence, and *shock*.'"

Patricia looked at her father and told him in a solemn tone, "Dad, now I want you to stand up."

Adrián obeyed her, smacking the air, because he expected a joke. But Patricia was serious. He had never seen her so grave. So respectable. She seemed to have grown up in just a few hours. As if the feast, the wine, the tiredness, the excitement had made her become a grown woman, far beyond her eighteen years.

"And this is *El País*, from Spain, Dad: 'Fifteen minutes were enough to put an end to fifteen years.'"

Bettini estimated that in the last few weeks there hadn't been a single night he didn't feel about to have a heart attack. Not now, *please*, he ordered his *fucking* heart. He swallowed saliva and, without even a smile, said to his audience, "*El País*, from Spain! *Se non è vero, è ben trovato.*"

39

"MR. FERNÁNDEZ. What an honor, Minister!"

"*Former* minister, Bettini. I've just gave my resignation, and I'm putting all my documents together to go home."

"Life takes many turns, Dr. Fernández."

"Sure. But don't think that this is the end of the story. You were able to make sixteen cats and dogs agree to support one candidate, some *Mr. No.* But now you'll have to make them agree on nominating one presidential candidate. They'll rip each other's eyes out."

"In this campaign we learned how to work together."

"Together? With duct tape and glue, Bettini. The real winner of this plebiscite is Pinochet, because the forty-something percent of the votes he got are for him alone. On the contrary, you'll have to divide your fifty-something percent among six-teen parties. With his forty percent, my general can do whatever he likes."

"Another coup d'état, like the one in 1973 against Allende?"

"Why not?"

"I don't think so, Minister."

"*Former!*"

"I don't think so, *Former* Minister. This time he can't count on the armed forces, or the support of the United States. And there's something else he had in 1973 that he doesn't have now."

"What is that, Bettini?"

"Someone to overthrow! Or will he be kind enough to overthrow himself?"

"My general will be remembered as a great democratic man. Tell me, what other 'dictator' called a plebiscite, and when he lost it, went home? Don't rest on your laurels, my friend. This little country needs to be managed with authority, not with silly songs like, 'It feels so good to say *No.*'"

"Why did you call me, Mr. *Former* Minister?"

"Ah, you're right. With so much nonsense, I forgot to tell you. Look, Bettini. Take a look out the window. You'll see a gray car without license plates . . ."

"Yes. I see it."

"Well, they're my boys."

"Yes, it's clear that they're your boys."

"How many are there?"

"Three, four . . . Perfect attendance. Gala day."

"What are they doing?"

"They're standing outside the car. One is smoking and the other ones are drinking water from plastic glasses. It's boiling hot around here."

"Well, please go and tell them they can leave. Tell them there was a change of plans."

"Actually, I don't have the slightest wish to leave home right now."

"Don't be afraid, Bettini. Tell them, 'Coco orders you to clear out.'"

"Coco orders you to clear out."

"*Ecco.* And everything's solved."

"I really appreciate your generosity. May I ask you why you're doing this?"

"When dinner is over, the dishes should be done. You scratch my back, and I scratch yours. We'll be in touch, Bettini."

FERNÁNDEZ HUNG UP the phone as if he were throwing off a stone. On the contrary, Bettini put the receiver back on the hook extremely slowly. Like in a trance. Exorcising something.

He was home alone. Standing in front of the hallway mirror, he tucked his T-shirt inside his pants. It was the old T-shirt of the Rolling Stones with the drawing of the red tongue sticking out. Moistening his lips, he tied his basketball shoes. It took him an eternity to run the laces through the eyelets.

"Coco orders you to clear out," he whispered. "How much longer will this nightmare last?"

He opened the door wide. The sun fell over his face, blinding him for a second. He held his right hand to his eyebrows, like a visor, and directed his gaze toward the men around the car on the other side of the street.

The one who was smoking threw the cigarette on the sidewalk and crushed it with his foot.

Another one put the plastic glass he was drinking from on the chassis.

The third man threw his cup on the sidewalk and then started to massage his right fist in the curve inside his left hand.

The last one kept drinking, almost indifferent.

"Out! Get out of here!" Bettini whispered, walking toward them.

And once he had them within reach, he stretched out his arm toward the horizon and emphatically told them, "Get out!"

40

THE PAY PHONE on the corner is available and I have a coin in my hand, but I don't make the call. I walk to our apartment thinking that I'm going to fix myself a tuna-stuffed tomato. At the grocery store, I buy some bread and an apple. I like the green ones because they're acid.

On the elevator, someone has written with a black marker, "We won, beauty." And on the other side someone scratched with a knife, "Nora." I start to open the door of the apartment when someone opens it from the inside. There, in the threshold, I see Patricia Bettini. She's wearing the uniform of her private school, that is, light blue blouse, blue tie, and plaid skirt with white kneesocks. It's weird. Every time I feel that something is weird, I pretend that I'm not surprised. I find it cool to be this way.

And there are reasons to be surprised—my friend never had the keys to my apartment.

But Laura Yáñez did.

And it's Laura Yáñez who now comes out from the kitchen and surrounds Patricia's shoulders with her arms.

She winks at me.

While I shake the key chain in my hand, two things happen—Patricia Bettini's mouth opens up in a smile that can't hide the imperfection of her middle tooth, which is slightly bigger than the others. And Professor Santos appears behind her, holding a cigarette between his lips.

No.

I'm telling the story wrong. First a puff of smoke appears and only afterward Professor Santos shows up, with a cigarette between his lips.

We hug each other in silence, and I probably take longer to release him than he to release me. So I think that he wants to look at me, and I move away a little and my old man asks me how I'm doing. I'm holding the green apple in one hand and the keys in the other, and I give him the same answer that I gave Valdivieso: "Still here."

In the dining room there are four seats and the starters are already served—ham stuffed in avocado on a bed of lettuce. Dad stretches his hand to put out his cigarette in the ashtray, and I see that his skin is full of burn marks. When he realizes that I notice it, he covers that hand with the other one and then rubs both enthusiastically, as if he were getting ready for a banquet. But I move away one of his hands and look carefully at his sores.

"There were no ashtrays in jail, and the boys would put out their cigarettes anywhere." He smiles. "Nothing serious, anyway. Everything as foreseen by the Baroque syllogysm.

"And you?"

"I'm great, Dad."

"Didn't you get in any trouble?"

"Zero problems."

"Today's the last day of the month. Did you go to pick up my check?"

"I forgot."

"It'll be interesting to know whether or not there's a check for me. I hope they didn't have the chance to stop it."

"I'll go after lunch."

"That's fine."

Patricia Bettini goes to the kitchen to get the bottle of red wine and my father takes out a tiny piece of tobacco that was stuck on his lip.

"She got me out," Dad whispers to me confidentially, pointing at Laura Yáñez with his chin.

"How did she do it?"

"You ask her."

"How did you get him out?" I ask without looking at her and hiding a smile while I fill Dad's glass.

She rubs her forehead with the cork.

Patricia strikes the table with her fist.

"She talked to people, Santos."

"With bad people, I suppose."

"Leave her alone, Nico," my father intervenes. "We're not living in the world of the Platonic ideals. In reality, Good and Evil are mingled."

"But in different proportions."

"In different proportions, son. Aren't you happy to see me?"

"Of course I am, Dad."

"Then?"

"It's all right."

"Let's eat, then."

IN THE AFTERNOON, I go to the payroll office. I wait in line for ten minutes. There's a check for Professor Rodrigo Santos. I take it and put it in my wallet. I buy the magazine *Don Balón* and see that it comes with a poster of two of my idols—Rossi and Platini.

I have philosophy class the following day.

Professor Valdivieso hands back the tests with his comments in green ink. He writes the grades in huge red letters. My Billy Joel song gets the highest grade, a B.

When I come back home, Dad asks me about my new philosophy teacher and I tell him that he's a good guy. I also tell him that he gave me a B for my test on the allegory of the cave. My daddy has a sudden fit of professionalism and wants to see my test. I hand it to him, and when he sees it, he leaves his cigarette on the notch of the ashtray. I take a puff and put the cigarette back where it was.

"What is this, Nico?" he asks, pale, after reading the Billy Joel song and seeing that the rest of the page is blank.

I don't know whether to laugh or cry.

"Justice to the extent possible, Dad," I reply, plucking the poster of Rossi with Platini out of the sports magazine.

41

SHE WANTS IT THAT WAY and I'm not going to refuse.

She asks me not to be insulted, but she will take care of the expenses.

She wrote a letter to Don Adrián and attached it to his pillow with pins.

It's not a matter of her being a silly, romantic girl like the ones in the shiny magazines, but she says that Santiago is wounded by the smog.

The buses to Valparaíso leave from Central Station.

I wasn't able to sleep a wink last night, and I'm afraid to get to the platform with a sleepy face.

I put a bathing suit and two apples in my backpack.

There are no clean towels left. If we go to the beach, I'll grab one from the hotel.

In the subway, I see Che yawning. I walk up to him and tell him that today I'll skip class. If they ask about me, he can tell the inspector that I have a cold.

He wants to know why I'm not going to school.

I give him a smile that might be contagious because he's instantly smiling just like me.

I have tons of sayings that I learned from Dad for this kind of situation—"Ask me no questions and I'll tell you no lies."

He wants to know if it's because of a chick.

It's not a chick, Che. It's Patricia Bettini. I'm taking her to Valparaíso.

I say, "I'm taking her to Valparaíso," but she's the one who's organized everything. She asked Doña Magdalena to advance her allowance and sold all her textbooks in a used-book store. "That's the advantage of not having younger siblings, Nico. Nobody at home will need those books anymore. I want to detoxify myself of everything—algebra, chemistry, history, physics . . .

"And virginity."

She said it like that, as if it were a difficult subject. She didn't say, "I want to detoxify myself of *my* virginity." She said, "I want to detoxify myself of virginity."

A few times we've been close to "breaking the scoreboard," as Julito Martínez, the sports radio announcer, likes to say. Both of us have read novels and poems that call for free love, and we have touched each other everywhere.

But she always found an excuse. She puts it this way, "Love is an expansion of a feeling of happiness. As long as a person is not happy, she or he shouldn't make love."

We were able to discuss all this very calmly when there wasn't a bed nearby. But alone in my apartment, or even in her bedroom when her parents weren't home, we've almost gotten to the edge of climax.

Also, of course, there was the issue of sadness.

Now she shows me a poem that she's underlined: "People have the right to be happy even if they're not allowed to."

Everything we've gone through has changed us a lot. It's as if we had to mature through blows.

She feels like living faster.

I want to caress and be caressed.

We want to be set free, she says, while filling a glass of grappa for me. Grappa is a drink just like pisco or brandy. But of course it's Italian. The bottle looks like a glass sculpture. The label reads GRAPPA MORBIDA.

It burns.

Che suggests that I stop by a pharmacy to buy rubbers. I'm not sure if I want that. I mean, I want to know what she's like. I want to feel her. And a rubber . . . Maybe I'm thinking like an idiot. I'll do whatever Patricia Bettini decides.

At the terminal, a voice announces that the next bus to Valparaíso will leave in ten minutes. The driver reads *La Cuarta* with his legs stretched out. The air from a small fan makes the pages of the newspaper shake. I take a look inside the bus, but I don't see Patricia.

I join the passengers saying good-bye to their relatives on the platform. A loader puts an old trunk in the luggage storage. He wears a headband with the drawing of a rainbow.

I fear that Patricia has changed her mind. For girls, the decision to make love for the first time is like something from a Greek tragedy. Or at least from a soap opera. They put so many things into their heads, both at home and school, that then they go through life walking on their tiptoes, trying not to break eggs.

And they're right. Love always leaves a mark on them. Even scars. That's why it's weird that Patricia Bettini has decided to be with me. We still have two months left before finishing high school. And Pinochet still has to call for free elections. That will take some time. Like one year, I think. She said to me, "I want to be with you, intimately."

But not in Santiago.

Santiago is the school, the church, Don Adrián's unemployment, the cars without license plates in front of her house, the tear-gas bombs, Professor Paredes's absence.

She wants me to understand.

It's fine. To me, loving her is not a matter of geography. Although I'm the least romantic guy on earth, I also like a place where the eye isn't always bumping into buildings and TV antennas.

I feel like being near the sea.

A sea to see her. Valparaíso.

But me, what's really me is downtown Santiago. I'm thrilled that the developers didn't knock down the colonial church and that they had to create a detour in the Alameda to preserve it.

"That's the way to treat a lady," Professor Santos said.

When they first announced that it would be demolished, my dad and I went out into the streets to protest along with the Franciscan priests.

My daddy delivered a speech near the fountain in the Pergola of Flowers.

He said that the church was the humble and sweet Francis of Assisi and the government of Pinochet was the wolf.

"Gubbio's wolf,"* he said.

I don't know where he gets those ideas.

---

* Gubbio is a medieval town in Umbria, where it is said that St. Francis tamed the wolf that terrorized its inhabitants.

He's bad at keeping quiet.

But he barely allows me to breathe.

So the cops came. First, they threw just a little bit of water at us. One gets used to their water. In the worst case situation, if the hose stream is too strong, it may push you against a wall and you may break your head. The best thing to do is to throw yourself to the ground.

So they can soak you. So they can leave you there drenched like a dog.

Professor Paredes used to say, bending down under the stream, "Relax and enjoy it."

Tear-gas bombs are a different matter. If one explodes in your face, you can end up blind.

But I've given all my life to downtown Santiago. Eighteen years. Lastarria Street. Villavicencio. The soda stands, with the vendor girls, with as much makeup as cabaret dancers.

Now the driver shouts that the bus will leave in three minutes.

I squeeze the hundred-peso coins I have in my pocket and try to see if there's a pay phone nearby.

Right at that moment, Patricia Bettini shows up.

And as she comes closer, running toward me, I feel my heart pumping stronger than ever.

It seems as if she's becoming smaller and slimmer inside my hug. Her brown hair falls loose on her shoulders and there's not a trace of the school discipline of bobby pins, headbands, and clips that she uses to prevent her hair from flooding over her face.

Today she's not wearing the school uniform.

She has on a tight red polo shirt, one size too small.

Her breasts protrude under the fabric, and she's showing cleavage.

Embellished with furious red lipstick, her lips perfectly match her shirt. It's a mouth screaming, "Kiss me, bite me." I swallow. I scratch her cheek with the few hairs that have sprouted in my chin. I breathe in deeply the smell of her skin. The aroma of tropical fruit from her hair gel makes me dizzy.

"Are you ready?" she asks.

She wants to know if I'm ready. I've set out on this flight. I live in the country of the *No*, and every one of my nerves knows that nobody will ever take it away from me. I feel it in the pulse of my wrists, in my temples, beating riotously.

In my erection.

Shoot! Democracy is so erotic!

"I'm ready," I say, only to not say all that's unutterable.

She puts the ticket in my shirt pocket and then touches my forehead with two fingers, like a doctor who needs to check if you have a fever.

"Then, Nicomachus Santos, your tickets to Valparaíso!"

42

PATRICIA BETTINI shows Nico Santos the notebook with a blue cover where her father was writing his notes for the *No* campaign.

A horse canters in the prairie; it's the horse of freedom.

A cab's windshield wipers move; it's the <u>No</u> of freedom.

A heart pumps, systole and diastole; it's the rhythm of freedom.

An old lady buys a tea bag at Don Aníbal's store; it's the tea of freedom.

A policeman hits a student on his head; it's the hour of freedom.

Song:

I don't want him, Daddy; I don't want him, Mommy; I don't want him in English, or in

Mapudungun; or in tango; or in bolero; or in fox-trot; or in cumbia or chachacha; I don't want him; I don't want him. What I want is freedom.

Christopher Reeve is in Chile. Film him— he came to protect the actors who have received death threats. Have him say something. Something like—"Okay, folks, you're right, remember that the vote is secret and that Chile being a free country depends on you."

Bravo, Superman; in English, he speaks of freedom.

Film Jane Fonda. I don't know where you may find her, but I heard her saying on the radio—"During all these years, the pain of Chile has been our pain, now the future of Chile is in your hands."

Let's include Jane with the boots song— "These boots are made for walking, and they will walk all over you; walk, boots; walk over Pinochet; walk, walk, walk, walk—toward liberty."

And let's use some cueca—"Tiquitiquití, tiq-uitiquitá, you say 'no' and freedom will light up."

And do not forget Violeta*—it gave me the alphabet, and with it the words that I think

---

* Violeta Parra (Chilean songwriter). What follows is an adaptation of her song "Gracias a la vida."

and declare; it gave me the "N" and gave me the "O"; it gave me the freedom to say "No."

They broke his hands, they fractured his femur; he was shot seventy-two times; they punched his belly. Freedom hurts. (No need to say whom we're talking about; everybody knows; it's better if people react by themselves.)

The cops don't allow Serrat to get off the plane. He shuts himself in the lavatory, and records a cassette with a journalist. "For Freedom" (play that song).

The young couple looks around; they collect coins and paper bills of very little value. They want to pay for a motel room. Freedom's cheap love.

Me, Bettini, I ask Death to wait for a while; we need to pass September. This is my last wish—after October 5, I won't ask for anything else. I only want freedom to wait with me for that date.

Girl dressed in black crosses Apoquindo Avenue. It's the height of spring and her thighs swing to the rhythm of freedom.

Over the head of the bearded king, a cardboard crown tilts; freedom is coming.

That hand waving <u>No</u> wants freedom.

A carpenter saws a piece of wood; the sawdust that jumps is freedom.

The woman in love plucks a daisy; freedom loves me, loves me not.

The first spelling book—Dad loves Mom; the boy loves his cat; the girl loves freedom.

No bird or angel flies higher than freedom.

The Pacific Ocean elevates blue cathedrals up to the clouds; waves up and down, toward freedom.

Don't tell me less, don't tell me more, tell me just the right word—freedom.

Let's see those palms, little ones, setting the beat, once more, clip, clap, clip, clap, once more, freedom.

Nico leaves Bettini's notebook on the motel room's nightstand.

But Patricia wants him to read one more time the prophecy—she uses this word—*The young couple looks around; they collect coins and paper bills of very little value. They want to pay for a motel room. Freedom's cheap love.*

She asks him to help her with her bra.

Nico unhooks it, as if he were an expert.

He's facing the back of the woman he loves. Her skin extends, pale, and for the first time he dares to touch with his lips a mole on her shoulder blade. The shoulder blade. Anatomy.

She turns toward him. Now her breasts are facing his mouth.

She seems to have sprouted up from that excited cloud floating outside the window.

She looks serious.

He smiles.

Together, they had put together the fifteen thousand pesos. A room for three hours. "Don't fall asleep, kids, or else I'll have to charge you an extra ten thousand. The two rum and Cokes are included."

Freedom, he thinks.

And his tongue climbs up her neck, all the way up to Patricia Bettini's mouth, and he sinks his tongue between her teeth.

She closes her eyes.

There has to be a way of doing it right.

A way to do it in style.

Like they had seen it in the movies.

Like they had imagined it so many times, amid wet sheets.

With the slow moaning, the swelling of the breasts, the erudite bulging of the virile member, the moistening of the belly, soaking it, his tongue must know how to find the exact spot, besiege it with the dexterity of a bullfighter, the planet's tiny electrified spot.

He has to stay calm; everything is too fast. His hands squeeze and scratch, jumping from one side to another other, like two scared rabbits.

It would be necessary to be thirty years old, and to be a skin expert, to have a doctorate in breasts, to give pleasure to the beloved Patricia Bettini, pale and warm under the faint daylight that filters through the flower-print curtain—daisies, sun-flowers, rhododendrons—in the oppressive shade of that hotel room, afflicted by an insolent sun that seems to want to set the port on fire.

Patricia leans against the padded green head-board, separates her knees, and lets the middle fin-ger and forefinger of her right hand go down her belly.

She caresses the spot, the instant, the glass of sparkling champagne, while her other hand goes to Nico Santos's nape.

Gently, but firmly, the other hand leads Nico's head to her belly, defeats him, and the young stu-dent obeys, brushes against her straight brown hair, and on this journey he breathes, deeply, the smell of her victorious secretions.

Skillful, he touches with the tip of his tongue the small tiger hidden in that abrupt vegetation, darker than it appeared in his dreams, a shade wilder than the most Italian, placid brown of her mane, and curled as from a sudden electricity.

Up to this point there hadn't been words, not even monosyllables, only the saliva on the skin, the rubbing of the thighs against the sheets, but now Nico Santos hears a word.

Patricia Bettini whispers "yes," and repeats "yes," and she says "yes" once and again, and "like that," "like that," and her fingers squeeze, electrified, Nico Santos's skull, and she doesn't say anything else, she doesn't say "yes," she doesn't say "like that." She remains ferociously quiet and focused, and she brutally clenches her teeth, and what Nico can't see, what he doesn't know yet, is that Patricia Bettini's crying.

43

PATRICIA DRAWS the printed curtain and opens the small window. The motel is high on the hill. She leans her forehead on the wooden window frame, tilts her neck, and looks out at the distance. The noises from the port sound stronger—cranes depositing huge crates on the ship decks, honks, ambulance alarms, the neighbors' radios playing the hits of the week.

"Come."

I walk over to her. She remains in the same position. Without looking at me, she takes my arm and puts it around her shoulders. She kisses my hand. It's weird, because she's far away and, at the same time, very much here. A divided body. Beautiful, loving, warm.

"Look," she says, scrunching up her nose a little bit and pointing at the hills. "If you want to know me better, I'm like them."

"What do you mean?"

"The hills and all that."

"You're like them."

"I was just saying, silly. Me," she says, tapping her chest, as if to mark the beating of her heart, "I'm this. I mean . . . if someone painted me and I were a landscape, I'd have many colors . . .

"Look here now. What do you see?"

"Many things."

"Roofs, roof tiles, yellow, green, purple, blue, red, brick-red walls, chimneys, seagulls, pelicans, stairs, steps, cables within easy reach, overhead tramways like small houses climbing onto the rails, stray dogs, kites, and everything remains there, as if someone had put it that way, thoughtlessly, leaving everything for later."

"And that's how you are? You left yourself for later?"

"I mean, all those things that have happened to me in my life have a meaning. They're here, with the same strong emotion that I felt at that moment, d'you know?"

"One of the things I like the most about you is that you almost never say *d'you know?* It's interesting, because I see you . . ."

I stop. I kiss her naked shoulder and breathe in deeply the smell of her neck. Going over her skin helps me find the exact word . . .

"How do you see me?"

"Harmonious, tanned. Elegant, Patricia Bettini. That's why I'm surprised to hear you comparing yourself with a carnival."

She turns toward me, and with two fingers she gently caresses my eyelids.

"Maybe," she says, smiling with her eyes but not with her lips, "it's the typical post-virginity-lost trauma. Do you know where my harmony comes from?"

"I talked about it with your father."

"Do you talk about me with my father!? What does he say?"

"That that's your 'Italian touch,' an internal commotion but a clear expression."

"Harmonious."

"Exactly, as if you had made a fair copy of yourself."

"And Laura Yáñez?"

"Laura Yáñez is a draft. Did you ever see the calligraphy notebook of a messy child?"

"Twisted letters, blots. But she saved your father, Nico!"

"I love her because of that. But I don't know if she'll be able to save herself."

Patricia looks suddenly serious. Almost grave. She signals me with her chin to look again at the road.

"Everything ends in the sea."

"I don't understand."

"You're always there and, at the same time, the infinite is there, too. If you're near the ocean, you put all those tiny everyday things in the infinite."

I exaggerate a yawn. "You should discuss these topics with Professor Santos. My old man is a fan of Aristotle and Anaximander."

"I don't get it."

"Anaximander is the oldest philosopher of all. Only a small fragment of his work remains."

"What is it about?"

"I know it by heart. 'Things perish into those things out of which they have their being, according to necessity.' And the dude became famous just with that tiny bit of philosophy."

Patricia walks to the table and takes her half-empty glass of rum and Coke. She tastes it and makes a funny face. It's warm.

"Shall I order some ice?"

"Just leave it. It's time for us to go back to Santiago. My old man must be looking for me to kill me. I left a note for him, attached with pins on his pillow."

Right after she says that, we hear a police siren, very close to the motel.

"That's him." She laughs.

"What kind of note was it?"

"One that, unfortunately, he'll know very well how to decipher. Three words: "Virginity, Valparaíso, Freedom."

She opens her thin lips in a charming smile. Oh, my God! I love her so much! I feel that I want her again.

"Do you like me?"

I shake my head.

"Not even a little?"

I nod. I don't like her at all. I frown my lips scornfully.

"Do you find me ugly?"

I nod enthusiastically. I find her hor-ren-dous.

Patricia Bettini draws the curtain completely. She shows her breasts to Valparaíso and sings at the top of her lungs.

E che m'importa a me
se non sono bella
se ho un amante mio
che fa il pittore
che mi dipingerà
come uns stella
e che m'importa a me
se non sono bella.

"Let's go back to Santiago," I say.
"Are you afraid?"

"A little bit. I don't think that Don Adrián would kill you. He's Italian and sentimental, so he would feel bad committing a filicide, but he wouldn't have the same scruples with me. At this very moment, I might be the number-one candidate on his hit list."

She opens her arms with a wild yawn accompanied by a deep "Ahhhhh." When she's done, she raises a didactic finger, like a rural teacher.

"Then I think that we'll all go back to the sea. I mean it, for Anaximander."

The rum is warm but I don't care. I drink it in one gulp.

"The *No* has driven us all crazy," I say while closing the window and taking a last look at the sea. "He's out of himself, he says yes, he says no, and no and no, he says yes in blue, in foam, in a gallop, he says no and no."

"Neruda?"

"The great Neruda. Or, as your dad would say, the *fucking* Neruda."

4 4

PROFESSOR SANTOS has never seen his son wearing a tie. They're going to walk together to the graduation ceremony. Before leaving the apartment,
he checks if he put a pack of black tobacco in the
inside pocket of his jacket, along with the Ronson
lighter, which has survived life's vicissitudes, and
which he refills every Saturday in a cigarette and
locksmith stand on Ahumada Place.

He then checks the knot of the green tie with
blue polka dots that Nico has borrowed from his
friend Che.

The event is taking place in the afternoon, but
neither the father nor the son changes his morning
routine. They leave the apartment and, before getting off the elevator, the philosophy teacher lights
his cigarette, takes Nico's arm, and smokes while

walking the two blocks to the gate of the National Institute.

There they will perform what is usually a routine practice, except that today it has special relevance: Nico Santos will graduate from high school with a more than acceptable average.

He was able to survive the turbulence of the dictatorship; he remained cautiously quiet, obeying not just his father's advices but also his strict orders. He's spoken out very few times, sometimes not so well, and sometimes okay, and sometimes very well, but in this last case he was prudent enough to do it in English. *"To be or not to be."* His son had opted for the *be*, and Professor Santos thanked his late wife for it. Certainly, the *not to be* would've ended up destroying him.

Then, with a histrionic gesture that reminds Nico of Professor Paredes's irony, he throws the cigarette butt on the ground, and bowing to his son, tells him that the prince may proceed to crush it with his shoe.

Nico Santos obeys with boundless joy. A triviality that he's happy to comply with. He draws his own conclusions, "The *No* won."

His father is alive. If he dies one day, it will be because of that stupid black tobacco and not the freezing cold of a prison cell.

Besides, his sperm had shot out like a big bang into the womb of the woman he loved. His experience proves that the world was created so that he could live his love with Patricia Bettini.

Today she's invited to the graduation ceremony. After his triumph with the campaign, Bettini has gotten new clients. The distributors of a French car have already given him their portfolio. At any rate, *Le Monde* had acknowledged his talent. *Ooh-la-la*. He bought his daughter a dress of the finest embroidered satin, open between the thighs like a mineral slash, with beads and Armani's unruly signature.

He paid more than he had, but he accepts that Pinochet was a genius when he put in circulation the credit card—that's the only way to get what you cannot afford. After him, the deluge.

Yet Adrián did this on one condition, which the girl humbly accepts—she has to wear the same dress at her own graduation ceremony, which will take place in the Scuola Italiana in three days. She better not dream of changing her wardrobe every two hours, as if she were an international movie star.

By the entrance to the auditorium there is a wreath of white roses, with some green leaves, and a few red carnations. Above, there is black poster board taped to the wall on which someone has written in yellow, "We don't forget our martyrs."

There are five names—two students and three teachers. One of them, Don Rafael Paredes.

As they walk into the auditorium, people pretend not to see the poster board. Since the triumph of the *No*, Lieutenant Bruna decided not to come back to the school. He sent the soldiers in a jeep to pick up his stuff.

The school chorus sings its anthem. Most students and guardians are singing it standing up. "Let it vibrate, comrades, the anthem of the institute, the song of the greatest national school . . ."

Nico Santos is one of the fifty-five young men who're graduating. The principal will hand out the diplomas one by one. Fifty-five times the audience will applaud, and the principal will have a picture taken with every student. Afterward, the photographers will be selling them to the relatives as they leave the school.

The students look weird in suit and tie. Their messy hair does not match the formality. Most of them are scratching their neck with their forefinger; others have loosened the knot of their ties. In the second row, Nico Santos and Che seem to argue about the probable outcomes of a soccer game.

Professor Santos and his special guests—Adrián, Magdalena, and Patricia Bettini—are seated in the third row. On their seats is a label that reads "Faculty member."

Professor Santos is a faculty member.

Professor Paredes was a faculty member.

In the second row, there is a seat with a card that can be easily read because the seat is empty: "Doña María, widow of Paredes."

". . . which had the astonishing fortune of being the nation's first spotlight," Professor Santos sings, without taking his eyes off Nico, who wipes his perspiration with the back of his hand. He's standing on the same stage where only a few weeks before, still a virgin, he performed in *The Cave of Salamanca*.

Bettini doesn't know the anthem. Moreover, his attention is now captured by the man who is approaching, resolute, despite the knees that block his way through the row, and walking toward him and gesturing him to make room. When the man gets close to Bettini, he sits with a satisfied sigh and, without looking at him, extends his hand to him.

It's Minister Fernández.

"How are you, Bettini?" he asks, adjusting the legs of his pants.

"Minister, what are you doing here?"

The man points at a dark-skinned boy with sharp cheekbones who waves at him from the stage.

Fernández answers by lovingly raising the fingers of his right hand, not higher than his neck.

"It's my grandson's graduation. My baby. Luis Federico Fernández. And you? What are you doing here?"

Bettini doesn't know how to respond. He comes up with something vague, "My son-in-law, I mean . . ."

"I know, your daughter's boyfriend. That's it, exactly that, your daughter's boyfriend. Meaning, Nicolás Santos . . ."

"No. Nico Santos. How do you know his last name?"

"Don't you remember, Bettini? The philosophy teacher, Rodrigo Santos . . . Did everything come out well?"

"Fine, Minister."

"*Former* minister, don't forget! And how's life treating you?"

"Well . . . I'm alive. Thanks to you, I suppose."

"Good heavens. You like to exaggerate!"

"I told your men to get the fuck out of there."

"Wow! How daring of you!"

"Not so much, Dr. Fernández. The construction workers in front of my place were looking at us."

"Even so."

Both applauded when the anthem ended and intensified the ovation when the principal came to the front to start his welcome speech.

"And you, what have you been up to lately, Minister?"

"Democracy is coming, my friend. I'm thinking about a position where I could practice my vocation to public service."

"As a senator?"

"I'd love to. I'm very good at creating projects, laws, all that stuff. Which one of the boys up there is your 'son-in law'?"

"The hairy one on the left, with a green and blue tie."

"I see. What's he going to study?"

"He wants to be either an actor or a writer. And your grandson?"

"Engineer. Like his father. Do you know that my son Basti voted for the *No* in the plebiscite?"

"Your own son?"

Dr. Fernández tapped his knees, cheerfully, with his fists.

"My own son. Democracy is wonderful, don't you think so?"

"Despite being 'a statistical exaggeration'?"

"Despite that. It's such a tender thing. Imagine— here we are, you and I, happy with life, looking together at the future of our nation. Me, next to my pampered grandson, and you accompanying the young Santos. By the way, I can't believe you beat us with such a stupid waltz."

"A stupid waltz, Minister?"

"A waltz super super stupid, Bettini! We can't deny it!"

"Dr. Fernández, are you familiar with *Actuel*, the French magazine?"

"What makes you think that? *Je ne parle pas français!*"

"They've just published an issue with all the songs that changed the course of history in the last fifty years."

"You're kidding! And they included the stupid 'Waltz of the *No*'!"

"Exactly, Minister. It's the 1988 song."

"And who were the other years' winners?"

"Jim Morrison, the Beatles, the Rolling Stones."

"And what are you creating right now?"

"No more songs, Minister. The next step is to win the elections with Olwyn and then send Pinochet to jail."

Fernández laughed so loudly that the audience looked at him. Even the principal gave him a look full of reproach.

"Hmm. I screwed up, it seems. To put Pinochet in jail?" he said in a low voice. "You won't be able, Bettini."

"We will, Dr. Fernández."

"No, no, no. It feels so good to say no . . ."

"Yes, yes, yes. We'll be able to do it."

"No, no, no. My general won't be touched, not even with a lady's petal."

Now it was Nico Santos's turn to receive his diploma. Patricia Bettini stood up and applauded, and the audience had the opportunity to admire her Armani dress. Adrián Bettini stood up, shouting, "Bravo," and Professor Santos scratched his head while holding an unlit cigarette between his lips.

Former Minister Fernández rose, too, and applauded Nico along with Bettini.

"We'll be back in power, Bettini," he whispered in his ear. "Step by step, little by little, one step at a time, one little vote at a time."

"That's the good thing about democracy, Minister. We had to earn it with blood, sweat, and tears, and you and people like you will able to enjoy it without the slightest effort. And one day, the statistical exaggeration will favor you instead. Those are the rules of the game. Good for you, Minister. All that matters is that you don't go around killing people."

"Don't dwell in the past, my friend. The crisis has been largely overcome. Do you remember when the people asked the armed forces to intervene and impose order? When they cried for a Pinochet?"

"Did you study at the institute, Dr. Fernández?"

"And proud of it! I belong to the Alumni Center Committee."

"Who was your Spanish teacher?"

"Don Clemente Canales Toro."

"So you surely studied the Archpriest of Hita with him."

"I remember it vaguely."

"A medieval author. Do you remember? Don Clemente Canales authored the modern Spanish version of the *Book of Good Love*."

"Sure! Very entertaining! There was a part called 'Praise of the Small Women,' right?"

"Bravo! And, by chance, do you remember the fable of the frogs? They were unhappy and demanded that the god Jupiter send them a new king."

"I don't remember."

"So Jupiter sends them a stork that eats two frogs at a time in a single gulp."

"Hmm. Where are you going with this story?"

"You'll see. The frogs that survive go to Jupiter and complain: 'The king you gave us because we foolishly asked you to gives us bad nights and very bad mornings.' Do you want me to explain the fable to you?"

Dr. Fernández brushed off some lint stuck on his lapel with his right hand.

"It's not necessary, Bettini. Like you said, democracy is a statistical exaggeration."

"*You* are the one who says that."

"That's true. Life is like a game. Now it's your turn to be 'it.' The challenge, if you win the elections, is to do something to overcome this naughty situation in which people are stigmatized, depending on whether they voted *Yes* or *No*. You must be modern and accept differences."

"You can accept whatever you want to. I won't. The rivalry between *Yes* and *No* will remain for a long time, because it's a matter of life or death. Those who think differently are either allowed to live or they're killed. I will never forget what happened."

"That's interesting. As for myself, I already forgot it."

"You're very modern, *Former* Minister."

The man started to applaud enthusiastically. Two beautiful hostesses were calling his grandson to receive his diploma from the hands of the principal.

Bettini wiped the palms of his hands on his thighs, raised them, and joined the minister in his applause.

"So, the fable of the frogs, Bettini."

"The fable of the frogs," Adrián Bettini repeated, applauding affectionately.